THAT WARRIOR

Life Viewed through Love, Laughter, and a Little Liquor

Thomas M. Caesar

ISBN-13: 978-1-7367077-2-2
ISBN-10: 1477123456

Cover design by: Art Painter
Library of Congress Control Number: 2018675309
Printed in the United States of America

www.thatwarrior.com

Dedicated to those who have joined me on my life's journey. Thank you. In the end, all we have is God (for those who believe), ourselves, our loved ones, our dreams, and our heroes.

Contents

Preface 1

1 That Guy 5
2 Two Olives In A Martini 8
3 It Always Boils Down To Food 15
4 Accelerating At xCellFitness 17
5 The Greeter 29
6 Ass To The House 38
7 Don't Mix Brands 40
8 Life Is about Love 44
9 Practice Makes Perfect 51
10 Sadness at the Celebration 53
11 Slow Progress 58
12 Good Meat 59
13 Unintentional Influences 63
14 True Beauty 68
15 Happy New Year 70
16 Trouble in Paradise 78
17 "You Ain't Woman Enough" 80
18 Nothing at All 88
19 What's the World Coming To? 91
20 Just This One Last Time 93
21 Heard It through the Grapevine 97
22 Alone In The Nest 100
23 Keep the Faith: Brian's Update 104
24 D-I-V-O-R-C-E 107
25 A Natural What? 109
26 Way of the World 112
27 PEE 114
28 Tuna and Butterflies 119
29 Colliding Worlds 124
30 Naked Pictures 128

31 You Gotta Do What You Gotta Do 130

32 Jack Discovers Love 133

33 They're Here! 134

34 P-Lee 141

35 The First Training Session 146

36 The Second Training Session 150

37 Behind the Scenes 154

38 Strike the Pose 158

39 Underdog Strikes Again 160

40 Ab Secret 162

41 Goodbye, Dear Friend 164

42 Rules of Engagement 167

43 My Turn to Help 169

44 Problem Solved 170

45 The Reality of Me 171

46 Dark Moments 175

47 Sunday's Family Spaghetti Dinner 181

48 Graduating to "After-Photo" Status 183

49 Prepping for the Show 185

50 Paving the Way 187

51 From Bad to Worse 189

52 Mirror, Mirror 194

53 Another Recruitment 197

54 Opposing Views 199

55 A True Miracle 202

56 A Revelation about My Heroes and Me 204

57 Did You Hear? 207

58 Karma's a Piss 211

59 P-Lee Ends 216

60 What I Was Thinking 219

61 It's Up to Me 224

62 The Late Show 229

63 Another Battle Over 230

Acknowledgments 235

About The Author 237

Preface

An Unconventional Book

I didn't set out to write a book, or to write anything else for that matter. After all, I didn't have a story to tell. Suddenly, a quartet of factors happened that changed my mind.

Sadly and unexpectedly, two people in my world passed away within four months of each other. Compounding the tragedy is the fact that they died young. In the weeks that followed their beautiful funerals, I couldn't help but wonder what meaningful life knowledge they would have shared if given the opportunity. When I pondered the question for myself, within days the foundation of my story was born.

At the time I was working for Marty, a man I greatly admire. Among Marty's many profound and thought-provoking statements, he mentioned that history repeats itself because human nature doesn't change through time. So while names and faces change, human nature remains constant. One day I realized that like human nature, personality types also transcend time. Television characters are the most identifiable examples of personality types. For example, we all know people who are lovable but somewhat dim witted, such as Gilligan on *Gilligan's Island*, Vera of *Alice*, and Rose of *The Golden Girls*. Then there are those who are sensible and levelheaded, like Louise Jefferson of *The Jeffersons*, Lamont on *Sanford and Son*, and Dorothy of the *Golden Girls*. The list can go on and on, but you get the idea. So Marty indirectly gave me the idea to base my characters on the universal and timeless personality-type technique. As a result, don't be surprised if my story has characters who exhibit your traits or traits of individuals you know.

The fourth and final situation that contributed to my need to tell my story is the extremely selfish, rude, mean, and self-centered actions bragged about on social media. I am just disgusted. To me, the news reported as jury journalism (my term for it) and social media posts serve as a measurement of the decay of the human race.

My Story

The daunting task of writing anything is probably a challenge for most but is especially monumental to me—a man with a limited vocabulary who's never written anything more substantial than an occasional Christmas letter. My vocabulary mainly consists of four-letter words—with my most frequently used words substitutable by an expressive finger gesture, my preferred mode of delivery. But I persevered thanks to using Google searches and the Google Assistant to identify and spell synonyms to augment, at least in print, my vocabulary. I am leaving it up to the editors to ensure I have selected the proper words, along with a laundry list of items to review and correct.

If you are expecting a story where some superhero, struggling with alcohol and drug addiction plus depression, runs after a plane on the tarmac, climbs into the plane through the wheel well, single-handedly kills the terrorists, and defuses their nuclear bomb before the meal service starts—all while going through drug withdrawal and without going to the bathroom—then you will be disappointed in this story.

Similarly, you will also be disappointed if you are looking for a formulaic book where the story's life cycle is based on the reader's progression through the book.

At its foundation, my story is about love and how love is expressed through actions as well as words. It is that simple. With such a sappy topic, I spiced up the story by including interesting characters and lots of sometimes questionable humor to keep the audience amused.

Decisions, Decisions, Decisions

Originally, I envisioned my story as a film and wrote an original script without having any film scriptwriting education or experience. Knowing no one in the industry, I had great difficulty finding a noteworthy film scriptwriter to convert my amateurishly written script into one that meets the industry standards and expectations. So, on the advice of a dear friend, I decided to convert the film script into a book. That's right, I converted an amateurishly written script into an amateurishly written book! Well, close but not quite. During the conversion to the book, I added many context-ual stories and descriptions as well as character revisions. I retained the film script qualities I felt were successfully communicated, like the crispness and the flowing character dialogue format, and I retained short segments (known as movie scenes, which translate to book chapters) to keep the intertwining story lines separated as they would be if naturally occurring. Each scene is a small window into a larger event and is used to express specific points or actions conducive to the story.

The film script to book conversion yielded a unique chapter format which followed the guideline of:

<Chapter Title>

Chapter introduction.
    Scene description.
                    <Character Name>
        Character dialog.
        (simple stage direction)
    Detailed stage direction.
Chapter summary.

My proofreaders got use to the format within a few chapters.

My story is full of characters who serve an acquaintance role in the main character's life. You know, the kinds of people you chat with at the gym, the bar, or at work. I faced a tough decision in deciding the level of character development to provide for such individuals. After all, how well do you really know these types of people? Probably not as deeply as you think. At least that's what I realized when using my own life experience as a guideline. As such, the characters are viewed from the standpoint of the main character, Tom, with only his limited knowledge and perception of these individuals.

Naturally, I am very grateful for the recommendations of the industry professionals and nonprofessionals I solicited. I carefully considered each recommendation, and I'm proud to say many improvements resulted. However, everyone has an opinion, and for my own sanity, the decision to act on a suggestion was left to my own intuition, even if that meant defying the experts and creating an unconventional product. Blame me, not the professionals. I guess you could say I am thinking "outside the book!"

Most Importantly, Thank You

Thank you very much for reading my story. I figure, if you're amused for a few hours, then I have met the basic entertainment goal. However, if through reading this book you improve your interactions with others, even by a single kind word or gesture, I will consider my efforts hugely successful and personally satisfying.

1 That Guy

We've already met. You remember. I was that guy who held the door open for you. I could tell you didn't expect it as you said "thank you" with an awkward smile. Last week in the supermarket checkout line, I was that guy who insisted you with your three items go ahead of me and my cart. When you dropped some change, I was that guy who picked it up and handed it to you. Or perhaps, that time when you were down on your luck, I was that guy who handed you twenty dollars outside the 7-Eleven. Probably a first and last for both of us. There were other times, too many to mention, but you recall that mannerly warrior. So you see, without realizing it, either directly or indirectly, we've already met.

Ah, you do recall but laugh at my claim of being a warrior. Well, there are many types of warriors with different appearances, agendas, and precepts. The warrior faction of which I am a member no longer lives, acts, or looks like our prehistoric ancestors. We warriors have progressed and modernized. We look like your neighbors because that's who we are. Our caves have been traded for apartments and houses. Thanks to Speedo and PETA, loincloths and hides are obsolete, thankfully exchanged for jeans, T-shirts, and even spandex for the more daring.

Repurposed and rebranded, our mission has taken on a broader spectrum. Gone are those chaotic, barbaric, rudimentary daily struggles for food and shelter. United in purpose, today our unwritten mission statement is to fight for the survival of goodwill in an increasingly selfish and self-centered society. We believe life is about love. And love manifests itself in actions as well as in words. It is that simple.

Unlike most other charitable organizations, we proudly transformed and operate without the need for telethons, fundraisers, subscriptions, tithing, government assistance, or membership dues.

Membership is open unconditionally to all. This means all races, genders, religions, creeds, sexual orientations, economic statuses, physical characteristics, and whatever other characteristics you can think of. We're always accepting new members; no one is declined. There's no application, qualifying test, secret membership oath, uniform, or logo. Since there isn't an operating manual to follow, adhering to and interpreting our mission statement while executing activities requires strict adherence to an honor system. Even if you were to use this book as a surrogate operating manual, you've still got to improvise as you go. Obtaining membership is easy, but retaining membership is tough. That's why we are an elite group.

Our medieval battle weapons such as the spear, ax, and sword have been replaced by the characteristics possessed by each warrior to fight for the *goodwill toward others*. There are eight possible warrior characteristics:

1. Manners (social grace, integrity, charity)
2. Management (organizational ability)
3. Mindset (dedication to cause and principle)
4. Motivation (ability to persuade or encourage)
5. Money (resources)
6. Muscle (strength, endurance)
7. Maturity (mental, physical)
8. Mobility (travel ability)

The count of each warrior's characteristics is known as the W-Factor. The maximum is a 8W; a good warrior is a 3W. In 99 percent of situations, such as opening doors and encouraging others, only the Manners characteristic, a 1W, is required.

We are beyond marking our participation or victories with trophies, ceremonies, certificates, awards, or prizes. Instead, we settle for the limitless personal satisfaction and fulfillment of helping someone with the hope that the recipient will join and help others in return.

As you see, we've evolved into something our primitive ancestors, and perhaps other warrior factions, would not recognize or comprehend. We are today's magnanimous warriors. Yes, we've come a long way, baby!

Every warrior has his own story. Now that you have insight into my mission, my story begins.

2 Two Olives In A Martini

It was 11:20 a.m. I was starved and annoyed. Very annoyed.

The bane of my professional life was Elaine, or at least Elaine as she existed in our work environment. We worked in a huge ground-floor room filled with waist-high worker cubicles. The cubicle walls were several inches higher than the desks, which meant everyone was visible from clear across the room when seated. Seeing everyone was one thing, but hearing their conversations was another.

Without a doubt Elaine was consistently the most obtrusive person in the room. Don't get me wrong, Elaine was a nice person. But she annoyed the hell out of me when she would sit on her desk or stand in her cubicle and, with a bullhorn broadcasting voice, attempt to teach her team of largely foreign workers about life in this country by telling her personal stories. If the stories had been conducive to their jobs, I would have managed. Had the stories been interesting, well, I could have managed. But they weren't. Every day my nerves were taxed.

It is nearly the end of a long, loud week. There was simply no relief, and I was on the brink of reaching my breaking point. Although I couldn't concentrate on work, I found I could concentrate on a solution to this noise problem. Since Elaine didn't know me very well, I didn't want to approach her directly. With something potentially as sensitive as this, I figured conveying a message to Elaine through a friend would be more effective. I had seen Cynthia and Elaine chatting a few times, so Cynthia, whom I hadn't met, would be the perfect person to tactfully discuss this topic with Elaine. Or so I thought.

On this particular morning, our coworker Jennifer, in the advanced stages of pregnancy with twins, enters the room. She has a laptop shoulder bag and various work documents in her hand as she slowly waddles down the long center aisle to her cube in the rear of the room. Prior to pregnancy Jennifer was cheerful and vibrant, the kind of person who draws an automatic smile to your face when she comes into view. Now, just one look at her and you immediately feel sorry for her. Her every step seems to be a struggle to find the strength to move each foot. The dark circles under her eyes indicate yet another night with minimal, if any, sleep. Her once cheerful disposition has now adjusted to her present situation of just getting by. I wonder why the doctor hasn't put her on complete bed rest; she looks exhausted. I am exhausted just watching her. As usual, Elaine can be heard in the background.

Jennifer is walking down the long aisle to her desk.

JENNIFER

Hi, Cynthia. Hi, Tom.

CYNTHIA

Right back at ya!

ME

How are the boys today?

JENNIFER

Very active. The doctor doesn't think it will be long before she meets them.

ME

That's great. I'm so glad you are having twin sons instead of twin daughters. I could never ask a woman, "How are your girls today?"

JENNIFER

(laughing as she struggles down the aisle)
I just love you.

ELAINE

Standing in her cube "teaching" her gathered team with a bullhorn-sounding voice.

> This weekend we are going to Spring Rock
> Campground. We've been going there since before
> we had any kids, so to my kids it's a second home. Of
> course, back in those days, we had a large tent and
> would do our cooking on a grill or portable kerosene
> stove. We'd sleep on air mattresses and have to use
> whatever washing facility the campground provided.
> Since there wasn't any air conditioning, we'd just suffer
> during a heat wave. We kept our food in a cooler and
> used purchased ice or ice packs.

Having reached my breaking point with Elaine's constant disruptiveness, I decide to execute my solution by heading to Cynthia's desk.

ME

> (at Cynthia's cube)
> Excuse me. We've never actually met. Cynthia, I'm Tom.
> Do you have a minute for a walk? There is someone I
> need to discuss with you.

CYNTHIA

> (looking at her watch)
> Sure. How about going to the cafeteria? It's opening in
> a few, and I like to get there before everybody hacks and
> hocks all over the food.

ME

> Great, let's go. I like to eat early. It's the highlight of my
> day.

Cynthia gets up from her seat and we head toward the room's exit. In the background Elaine continues her educational session.

ELAINE

> My kids love to go camping. So we take them as
> often as we can. We keep a bag containing games like

Life, Trouble, Yahtzee, Battleship, Operation, and
Monopoly. At night we all sit around the campground
picnic table playing games. It's relaxing. Today we own
a twenty-five-foot trailer that sleeps eight and has an
indoor toilet with a shower. Back in the day some of
the campgrounds actually had outhouses for toilets. An
outhouse is an enclosed building with a deep hole in
the ground covered with a wooden box that is used as a
toilet seat. Sort of like going to the bathroom on a bus.
Sometimes I need to use our camper's shower for storage
and make everyone use the campground showers. Now
I no longer need to worry about maintaining ice or ice
packs once we've set up camp because the camper has a
refrigerator with a freezer. Some of my friends' parents
are starting to go into a nursing home. In this country
when adults need supervision, it seems they are pushed
off into some sort of home. But my parents are still in
good health, so we take them with us camping. They
play board games with my kids. Everyone has a great
time.

Thankfully Elaine's voice is not heard once we exit the double doors
into the corridor. We head directly to the cafeteria. Fortunately, the
corridor is wide enough that we can walk side by side and still let
others pass. We talk as we walk.

CYNTHIA

So what did you want to talk about?

ME

I've seen Elaine chatting with you a few times, so I
figure the two of you are friends. I don't know how to
ask you this, but is there any way you can get her to
shut up? Her nonstop talking is so annoying I can't
concentrate on my work.

CYNTHIA

Oh, I know. Isn't it awful?

ME

I think she has Restless Mouth Syndrome!

CYNTHIA

And if I have to hear about her bag of games one more
time! I don't see that we can do anything about her. Let's
just hope they move her or us. What are you getting for
lunch?

ME

I usually get the soup and the salad bar, but they give
me wicked gas. I even mentioned it in the food services
survey, although I doubt anyone will read it.

We arrive at the cafeteria just as it opens. Although open, not
everything is set up, and the workers are busy with their last-minute
preparations. We are the first two customers that day.

CYNTHIA

I'm skipping the salad bar today. I don't need a colon
cleansing. I'll get a sandwich instead. One second while
I place my order.

I follow Cynthia to the sandwich station. Marie, an older lady, is
behind the counter still setting up. There is a large, industrial-size
plastic wrap box on the ledge above the counter.

CYNTHIA

Hi, Marie. Could I have my usual to go?

MARIE

No problem. How's Cynthia?

CYNTHIA

Fabulous.

Cynthia leads me to the soup station. She lifts the lid on the large
soup pot.

CYNTHIA

Here's the secret: To minimize the intestinal issues,
you've got to get the food right when they put it out.
Especially the soup, unless you want a cup of broth.

Cynthia takes the ladle, stirs it around in the large soup pot, and raises the ladle above the pot's surface to inspect the broth for substance.

CYNTHIA

People like to pull out the meat and vegetables from the
soup because it's cheaper to buy a cup of soup than it is
to weigh it from the salad bar!

Cynthia nods her head with approval, indicating there is acceptable substance within the broth. I follow Cynthia to the salad station.

And when you select from the salad bar, you've got to
take from the bottom (picks up tongs to demonstrate)
where it is colder. Not from the top where the warm
air gets it. And don't even think about a salad after one
o'clock unless you want to blast off from your desk
(laughing).

I reach for a salad container.

ME

Interesting, I never realized any of that. I hope they have
chicken breast.

CYNTHIA

(looking at me like I'm crazy)
Are you serious? They serve only the cheapest chicken
meat here.

ME

Which part is that?

CYNTHIA

(laughing) Chicken butt.
I'm going to pick up my sandwich. See you at the
cashiers. If you have the time, let's eat here. It'll be a lot
quieter.

ME

And cooler. Most of these summer days I sit at my desk
moist.
(looking at the clothing of a passing person)

Fortunately, I wear natural fiber clothes. I don't know
how some people cope.

At the sandwich station, Marie is struggling with the plastic wrap.
The industrial-size container is too large and heavy for her to move. It
is also too high and facing out to the customers instead of facing her.
Marie has to perform an extended outward reach several times to pull
the plastic wrap. This action causes her chest to swing back and forth
over Cynthia's sandwich. Cynthia sees Marie's chest swinging over her
sandwich as she approaches.

CYNTHIA

Wouldn't it be easier to spread the mustard using a
knife?

MARIE

(laughing)

You always make my day, Cynthia. Here you go.

Marie hands the sandwich tray to Cynthia. We pay and head into the
dining area to enjoy our first meal together.

Even though my plan to recruit Cynthia to talk to Elaine about her daily
disruptive conversations had failed, something better happened: the birth
of a wonderful friendship.

3 It Always Boils Down To Food

You can pick your house, but you can't pick your neighbors. As it turned out, I got fortunate with Sheila and Howard. Both Sheila and Howard live across the street from me next to each other. Howard and I are the same age, and Sheila is about ten years older, though thanks to her rigorous workouts and healthy diet, she looks younger than us. Sheila would say much younger.

Then there was Jack. I was scared to death of Jack from the minute Sheila introduced us. At first I thought Jack was a German shepherd; later I learned he is actually an Akita. In Sheila's backyard, he looks regal and peaceful—peaceful, that is, until a stranger approaches. Then Jack goes into attack mode with his ferocious barking and strategic positioning nearest to the intruder, as he protects the backyard from potential unapproved visitors.

Like my neighbors, I love pets. I wanted to be able to pet and play with Jack, but he seemed too mean. I wondered … if the way to a man's heart is through his stomach, would this same strategy work on a canine? It seemed reasonable enough, so my weekly grocery shopping included an additional item—cigar-size, peanut-butter-filled premium dog treats.

I'm crossing the street to Sheila's house. Another neighbor in his yard sees me.

MALE NEIGHBOR

Hi guy, what are you up to?

ME

Going to visit Jack. I'm trying to get him to like me by
feeding him premium dog treats.

I hold up the cigar-size dog treat as I walk.

MALE NEIGHBOR

I'd like you if you fed me that.

As I approach the fence, Jack is already there in attack mode,
barking furiously.

ME

Here you go, Jack.

I hold a dog treat above the fence. Jack puts his front paws on the
fence and extends his head to grab the treat. I stand back for safety.
Jack takes the treat in his mouth, leaves the fence, walks several feet
away, and eats it.

ME

Ah, good puppy.

Like many times before, when Jack finishes, he resumes his spot by
the fence—paws on the ground—and recommences attack mode
until I have left the property and am in the street.

4 Accelerating At xCellFitness

It wasn't like I woke up one day and decided to join a gym. There had been previous attempts to get into shape. Most notable were the times I'd used the college gym. I'd go late at night when I didn't think anyone would be there. Okay, I used it exactly twice, and both nights it was just me and the same athletic, muscular student. The second night the guy asked me to stop because I was disrupting his workout!

A few years later, I got my first apartment. I purchased a bench, bar, and weights. It didn't occur to me to start lifting with light weights—maybe five or ten pounds or with no weights at all. Foolishly, I tried to lift the bar with two twenty-five-pound weights and nearly managed to kill myself on the first and only lift. Not only were the weights far too heavy, but without the weight-securing barbell clamps, the weights slid along the bar and eventually fell off as I struggled to hold the bar parallel and prevent it from crashing down on my chest. This one incident scared me half to death to the point where the equipment sat idle in my living room for two years. I placed it on the curb when I moved.

Years later I was in a bookstore with a coworker who found a work-out book she had heard offered a successful body sculpting program. Unlike the other books, this book had photos of the individuals who utilized their workout program. For each individual, there was a "before" photo taken prior to program initiation and an "after" photo taken upon program completion. We stood in the bookstore amazed over the transformations. The lucky people in the before pictures looked ordinary; the not-so-lucky people, which to me represented most of the candidates, reminded me of the villains in a horror movie. Astoundingly, these same individuals changed into someone who could easily pose for *GQ*, *Vogue*, or any other fashion magazine. I never realized working out could make such a difference. I wanted to look like those in the "after" photo. If they could do it, so could I. This time I was serious and determined.

xCellFitness is a hard-core gym, not a social gym. At least it was prior to me joining. Luckily, the gym is located about three songs away from my house. That is just far enough that I couldn't use the length of the car ride as an excuse not to go. It is in a terrible location—a decaying shopping center with maybe three open and twenty-five vacant stores. Across the street are a housing project and low-rent apartments. The decrepit shopping center serves as a playground for the neighboring kids and a secluded spot for drug deals. This was a foreign world to me, the kind of area where I probably shouldn't be at all, especially not after dark.

The inside of the gym appeared not to have been renovated since it opened nearly fifteen years prior. The gym reeked of fitness: the front counter glass displays contained many impressive trophies won by its members. The interior walls were lined with both black-and-white and color photos of famous male bodybuilders like Arnold Schwarzenegger, Lou Ferrigno, and Lee Haney. Truth be told, I only knew two of the more than dozen famous male bodybuilders whose pictures hung on walls. Posters promoting tanning supplies and various fitness products such as energy drinks, protein bars, and powders comingled on the walls along with posters providing motivational encouragement. Quite frankly, I found the models used in the motivational posters more inspiring and memorable than the actual slogans.

The place also reeked of flesh. Almost everywhere I looked there were gorgeous specimens of the male physique—muscular, hulking guys in their twenties and thirties who were probably on steroids. The hulking guys attracted beautiful young women with big hair and airbag-size breasts. Now, these weren't dainty ladies parading around the gym in their compressed clothing hoping to catch the eye of a beefy guy, although there were a few of them. No, these ladies were determined; they worked as hard or harder than the guys. Yes, these women were my tough competition, and as I got to know them, I told them just that!

After I was a member for a while, I realized that the gym members, quite surprisingly, ranged from low income to the upper 1 percent. I was told xCellFitness had the best bodybuilding equipment in the area. I also heard there was an agreement with the police department for free or reduced memberships, which meant it was safe to be in the immediate parking lot and inside the gym. Even when there weren't off-duty police members present, for reasons that probably defy logic, the gym was amazingly harmonious.

Being serious about bodybuilding meant I had to be at xCellFitness. Once I signed up, I was entitled to three free sessions with a personal trainer. Given my previous bodybuilding attempts, I decided not to start using any of the equipment until I understood how to properly use it, which I hoped to accomplish during my free sessions. Tonight was the first session with the trainer. It also marked the first time I used the gym. I was scared and intimidated.

I enter the gym, go directly to the counter, and wait behind a lady probably five years younger than I.
VANESSA

(speaking with a no-nonsense attitude to the front counter person)
It's the usual. Bottle of water and I'll pay for my shake in advance.
(leaning inward to get a better view of the floor behind the counter where an employee's dog's dishes are located)
Is that a mouse eating out of Raymond's food dish?
ME

You've got to be kidding.
VANESSA

(speaking matter-of-factly)
Look, around here if you don't pass out from the sight of mice, you will from the urine smell.
Vanessa walks off after getting her bottled water, shake card, and

change from the counter worker. I like Vanessa immediately. She is
a tough, efficient, take-no-crap-from-anyone type of person. With
her razor-sharp tongue and quick thinking, she can right-size anyone
from disillusionment to reality in a heartbeat. Later I learn she is a
nurse for a charitable organization that ministers to the homeless,
and she is perfect for it. Vanessa questions, observes, and remembers
everything. Even her least-intelligent staff member and patient have
to quickly realize Vanessa is not gullible. Her appearance matches
her personality: not ostentatious. Vanessa's hairstyle was simple,
classic, and neat atop a face that rarely wears makeup. She dresses in
appropriate gym clothes that did not reveal or embellish her cleavage.

ME

(to the counter person)
I'm here to see Drew for my new-member orientation.
The appointment is for six o'clock.

FRONT COUNTER WORKER

You're early. Drew is finishing up with his client. If you
have a seat at the table, I'll inform Drew that you're
here.

ME

Thank you very much.

I walk over to the round table and take a seat. Two muscular
and hulking bodybuilders, Lee and Ted, were already at the table
immersed in conversation. They do not acknowledge me. I am
delighted to be sitting at the table with two such attractive guys. Not
wanting to stare at them and to appear like I am minding my own
business, I start looking around inside the gym while they talk.

LEE

Megan says I need to shape up or ship out.

TED

Oh, you can hear that fifteen to twenty times before you
need to worry.

LEE

My parents said I can move into their basement if I need to.

TED

I don't think it will come to that.

Ted and Lee grab their belts, workout gloves, and gallon water containers and leave the table to work out. Seated alone at the round table waiting for Drew, I became even more aware and intimidated by the surroundings. Sounds of weights clinking, dumbbells dropping, and various noises from treadmills, stair climbers, and elliptical machines occasionally overpower the broadcasted rap music. These are foreign sounds to me, especially the rap music. I prefer country music—by musicians like my heroes Conway Twitty, Tammy Wynette, George Jones, Dolly Parton, Reba McEntire, Tanya Tucker, and, of course, my all-time favorite, Loretta Lynn.

Huge guys are working out in groups across the gym. One twenty-something-year-old woman is oddly blocking an aisle doing stretches on the floor. With mice present I would not recommend that. Over on a treadmill, a young guy, possibly ex-military, with serious mobility limitations slowly adjusts the treadmill settings to exercise his service dog. It's heartbreaking to watch him program the equipment.

Suddenly, my attention is drawn to Zeke, a man in his twenties wearing gray sweatpants that reveal a bulge so huge that when he walks it seems to arrive two seconds before the rest of his body. I'm not sure if it's obscene or gross, but either way it is hard not to stare and envy.

In my nervousness I begin wondering if I had made a mistake joining this gym. I am deep in thought when I am startled back into reality by the sound of my name.

DREW

Mr. Caesar.

Drew extends his hand, which I shake.

I am glad you decided to purchase a membership. Let's go to my desk where we can talk. Please follow me.

Drew is a middle-aged, married trainer with a level of class, experience, and professionalism that rises above that of the establishment and its location. He is tan and very toned but not muscular. Within the first several minutes, through Drew's interactions with me, I realize Drew is a man of substance. I like him, especially his warmth, integrity, charisma, and outgoing, nonthreatening style. I can tell he is a wonderful father.

ME

Please call me Tom.

DREW

Tom, with your membership you are entitled to three one-hour sessions with a trainer. With this being your first free session, it will be divided into determining your fitness experience level and goals, discussing your dietary experiences, and doing some basic fitness exercises to baseline your progress.

I've reviewed your health survey and everything appears to be fine. So please tell me about your fitness goals and experience. Have you ever belonged to another gym?

ME

Yes, I joined the Y for a year. It was too far from my house so I never went.

DREW

Do you think you'll have the same problem here?

ME

No, this is much closer to home.

DREW

I see you live in Pawtucket. There are several gyms in the area. What made you select xCellFitness?

ME

The guys at the bar were eager to tell me what happens in the locker rooms of those other gyms. I don't want any part of that. So when I inquired about this gym, nobody said anything. That's when I knew this would be the gym. Looking around, it looks like a rough place.

DREW

Don't let anyone intimidate you. You'll find some very nice people here. So then you don't work out?

ME

I did Weight Watchers and lost sixty pounds in six months all without exercising. I actually got too thin, and my friends thought I was sick. Then I started the Body for Life program to get toned. Are you familiar with it?

DREW

Yes.

ME

I spent three thousand dollars and converted half of my two-car garage into a gym. Complete with air conditioning and kerosene heaters. My utility bills were enormous. I had the most comfortable insects in the neighborhood. After a year, I decided it was time to go to a professional gym before my utility bills bankrupted me or my garage burned down.

DREW

So your goal is to get toned?

ME

Yes, I don't think I am too far off.

DREW

We have several trainers, myself included, who can help

you reach your goal. And we can offer you a diet plan. A proper diet is a key to being in shape. We offer half-hour and full-hour sessions. Our programs and rates are listed in the welcome packet. In addition, we have several nonstaff trainers who have their own agreements with the gym. Usually they will find you, but you'll see them training their clients on the floor. Feel free to walk up to any of them and ask for more information. Some people use a trainer not only for the training, but also for support and motivation.

ME

Thank you. The only support I need I get from my undergarments. I'd like some basic understanding of how the machines work. If I don't feel something is working or could be better, I will reevaluate and make the necessary changes.

Drew leads me to the leg press machine.

DREW

Sit here.

I sit on the seat.

DREW

Some people like the machines best because they usually focus on one muscle group at a time, and the motion is exact for that muscle group. It is very important you make all the seating adjustments properly for the machines to be effective and avoid injury.

Drew adjusts the seat and seat back.

DREW

All of these machines are synchronized, so whatever setting number you select for one machine will be the same number on a different machine for the same part. Every piece of equipment shows the starting and midpoints of the motion. From the midpoint, return back to the original start. Remember to exhale when

your body is working hard and inhale on the easy part
of the motion. If you don't breathe properly, your body
will be starved of oxygen, and you will become light-
headed or dizzy.

I try, taking it slowly and paying attention to the breathing.

DREW

Again.

We walk to an area with mats, and Drew asks me to do sit-ups. As I
struggle, Drew counts.

DREW

Two.

Three.

Drew's attention wanders, and he laughs. I stop and look at Drew.

ME

Please don't make fun of me. I'm doing the best I can.

DREW

Sorry. I wasn't laughing at you. I was laughing at the
member interactions.

Sitting upright, I look in the direction where Drew is facing. I only
see mirrors.

ME

There's no one over there.

DREW

I was watching a couple on the other side of the gym.
Using the mirrors, you can see people all over the gym,
and they will never know you are looking at them.

I am skeptical of his explanation.

The gym is a lot like a bar, only better because you can
see people in revealing clothing, which takes the edge
off (quick laugh).

ME

I briefly study the mirrors in proximity, but I only see workout
equipment. I am not able to conclude if Drew's claim of seeing people
all over the gym is valid, but it does intrigue me.

That's good. It's hard to meet people in Pawtucket.
Perhaps I will find someone here.
                    DREW
Come on, back to work. We're almost finished.
The lady who blocked the aisle with floor stretches jumps up on a half
wall near us. Using the half wall as a balance beam, she performs an
aerial cartwheel and, with great accuracy, concludes several feet away
still atop the half wall. We are in awe. She jumps down and exits our
area without acknowledging or making eye contact with anyone.
                     ME
That's impressive.
                    DREW
Yes. That's our Megan. I admire her talent and tenacity.
This is her gym.
Drew leads me over to the cardio area and asks me to get on a
treadmill between two young ladies. One of them is Vanessa, who was
ahead of me in line when I entered the gym.
                    DREW
It's very important to exercise your heart. See the
button that says, "Quick Start"? That's the fastest way
to engage the machine if you don't want to answer all
the questions or set a program. I suggest you do twenty
minutes of cardio daily. A brisk walk is fine. There is a
clip that should be fastened to your clothing that when
pulled away from the machine will stop it. Otherwise,
you can always press the Stop button. Do you have any
questions?
                     ME
No.
                    DREW
This will conclude your first session. When you are
ready for a second session, the front counter person will
schedule it. Let me introduce you to Vanessa and Judy,
two of our members.

(to Vanessa and Judy)
This is Tom, he is new.
JUDY and VANESSA
Hi.
From atop the treadmill, I smile and nod at Vanessa and Judy.
ME
(to Drew)
Thank you very much.
I shake Drew's hand. He departs the area.
VANESSA
How did you make out?
ME
Well, I didn't pass out from the urine smell or the mice.
JUDY
Just give it time.
Several African American demigod bodybuilders walk by.
DEMIGOD 1
(to the other demigods)
Can you believe the lady locked her doors when she saw
me walk between the cars to get to mine?
DEMIGOD 2
Still stereotyping us!
ME
(leaning toward Vanessa but loud enough for Judy to
hear too)
If it were me in the car, I'd be *unlocking* it!
JUDY
I need to introduce myself to them.
VANESSA
(speaking in true matter-of-fact style)
The first one is Jerry. He is a cop.
ME
Am I too old for the PAL (Police Athletic League)?

And so concluded my first day at my new gym. Overall I was very pleased with the way things went. I didn't get injured or make a fool of myself. Drew's comment about watching people using mirrors fascinated me. Most interestingly, there was only one seating area in the gym, and that was at the round table. That table served a multitude of functions including a waiting area, pre- and post-workout spot, and an area to consume your food and/or beverage. Most importantly, I met three nice people who would help make my return visits less horrifying during my attempted "after-photo" transformation.

5 The Greeter

For many years I ignored gay bars for fear they were seedy, unsafe, and dirty. During my first visit to Equilibrium, I realized how wrong I was.

Larger cities tend to have multiple gay bars, with each bar having a theme, such as sports, collegiate, or bikers. It works out great because you can be with others who enjoy that same atmosphere.

However, I live in a small city with just one gay bar—Equilibrium. As such, it draws all the gay demographics throughout the various hours of the night. Early evening brings a mixture of older gays and gay-friendly individuals who stop in for happy hour after work. Within an hour or two the middle-aged guys enter—perhaps a drink or two after dinner to catch up with the other locals. Then, by eleven o'clock, the young crowd joins in for festivities such as dancing or drag shows. As for the themes, well, you come dressed as you like, which ensures a wide range of appearances.

Having just one gay bar typically means there is a small gay community. It also means that everyone knows or knows about everyone else. Very little occurs without being broadcasted, often inaccurately, to the rest of the group. Eventually, you get used to the rumors and gossip. The smart exhibit good social grace because you can never escape running into an ex.

Equilibrium's main bartender is Lyle, a middle-aged, attractive gay man who has been on the scene for two decades. He is known to all and is discreet about the vast people knowledge he has collected. Lyle has the "pour and go" bartending mentality—after he serves your drink, you are left alone for your own entertainment while Lyle plays on his phone or talks to his friends. The lack of a socializing bartender, combined with the fact that the community can be very cliquish, results in the bar being a very lonely place for first-time visitors, even when the place is packed.

I only go to the bar on weekends, i.e., no weekday happy hour for me. I arrive early and leave before ten or eleven. Sometimes I am the only customer for the first hour. Since I have known Lyle for years, he is less standoffish toward me. If there are customers at the bar who appear to be alone, I will introduce myself and initiate conversation just to make them feel welcome. Call me "the greeter."

Inside Equilibrium. It is far too early for the late-night, young dance crowd and those looking for a quick hookup. The phone rings. Lyle answers it.

LYLE

Equilibrium.
(long pause)
No, they aren't here.

I know Lyle is referring to Arnold and Randall. These two men can make an hour bar visit seem like the passing of a slow week. They can be very loud, disruptive, and rude to the point that some individuals avoid them in the bar, while others avoid the bar altogether knowing they are there. It is very sad to watch grown men act this way. It's even sadder observing the annoyed looks of other patrons during their act.

I see one person in the bar and head for the barstool next to him. Nearing, I realize it's a man in drag, but the drag effort seems somewhat incomplete without any makeup, shaved body, or wig. His large, masculine frame with a short haircut and hairy body seems contradictory for someone wearing a dress. Don't get me wrong: I'm describing, not judging. Giving makeover critiques is inherent to a gay guy. His transformation tonight seems to be still in progress. Perhaps he needed a drink before he could proceed; we've all been there.

ME

Hi, I'm Tom. I see it's a typical Saturday night here in
Pawtucket. You look great.

Man-in-Drag is nursing his almost depleted drink.

The dollar bills on the bar indicate he has been there awhile.

MAN-IN-DRAG

Thanks.

ME

Is that your car out there?

MAN-IN-DRAG

Yes.

ME

The Porsche 911 is a great car. Do you like it?

MAN-IN-DRAG

Love it.

LYLE

(to me)

Are you having the usual?

ME

Please.

(referring to Arnold and Randall)

Do you think they're coming in tonight?

LYLE

No, I think we are safe. But give it another fifteen
minutes to be sure.

ME

I hope not. I don't feel like dealing with them tonight.

For several years, whenever I was in the bar with Arnold and Randall,
I would intentionally visit with them just to provide a temporary,
tranquil environment for the customers and staff. To reduce the
risk of them getting loud, rude, or argumentative, I ensured our
conversation topics were always trivial and noncontroversial.
Disappointingly, during my last visit with them, one of them
disagreed with my opinion in such a rude and condescending

manner, I abruptly left them and immediately stopped all future goodwill visits. The goodwill flame is extinguished.

LYLE

It's not like you to be uncharitable.

I shrug my shoulders.

I notice another customer off in the distance lurking in a dimly lit area. It is a bearded man. He also sees me. I notice him several times during my conversation at the bar.

ME

(to Man-in-Drag)
What do you drive in bad weather?

MAN-IN-DRAG

An Audi Q7.

ME

Very nice. Your cars must be expensive to maintain.

MAN-IN-DRAG

I do all the maintenance myself. I'm a mechanic.

ME

Wow.

LYLE

Do you want to cash out or start a tab?

ME

Can you wait about twelve minutes? Should they come in tonight, I'm no longer taking one for the team. The last time I did, Arnold told me that although I am usually "on point," that night I wasn't and he proceeded to tell me why with his provincial knowledge and in his patronizing style. The actual point that he continuously fails to see is I only go over to talk to them to distract them for ten or fifteen minutes, to provide a nicer environment for everyone else.

LYLE

They are out of control. One bartender downtown

threatened to tinkle in their drinks if they don't stop
acting up.

ME

That's sick. But I guess it's more satisfying than spitting
into it.

LYLE

I heard about the Loretta Lynn concert last weekend.
Cody was telling us that when he had a front-row seat at
the Loretta Lynn show in Boston, Loretta was looking
to him for the words to her songs. I almost laughed in
his face.

ME

Truth be told, just about anyone in the audience could
have given them. But she didn't need any of us.

As I am speaking, I notice a young guy entering the bar and holding
a dress and Styrofoam wig head. The guy pauses at the bar just as I
finish my comment.

LYLE

(loudly to the Show Contestant guy)
Changing room is back to the left. There is a sign on the
door. Let me know if you have any questions.

Show Contestant nods and keeps walking.

ME

I don't like drag shows. Last time I stayed too long
Barbara asked me to judge. Each minute was eternity.
To me, they are Ethel Merman look-alike contests.

With such comments you can clearly see that I struggle with certain
portions of the Manners characteristic. But I am working on
improving.

LYLE

That's not nice. Some of these drag queens do shows in
Boston and New York City.

ME

I applaud their guts and in some cases nerve. Perhaps

if I saw a drag show in a big city I would like it. I like
masculine guys.
(turning to Man-in-Drag)
Are you staying for the show?

MAN-IN-DRAG

No, I'm leaving soon.

A second guy, who is older than the first, enters the bar. He is
carrying drag show supplies, such as a makeup kit and shoes.

ME

I don't know who that guy is, but if that's his boyfriend,
he is certainly robbing the cradle.

LYLE

It's his father. He helps his son at all the shows.

Man-in-Drag and I look at each other, clearly surprised.

ME

I bet when his son was born, he never thought he'd be
helping his son look like a woman.

MAN-IN-DRAG

Mine never would.

ME

He gets my vote for Father of the Year.

MAN-IN-DRAG

(starts taking excess cash off the bar and putting it into
his wallet)
Gentlemen, have a nice weekend.
(departs)

ME

I'm cashing out too.

By this time, more show contestants had arrived to prepare. It is
time to leave. On my way out, I approach the bearded guy that I'd
observed several times. He is dressed in a flannel shirt underneath
jean overalls and wears his hair short. As I walk I realize it isn't a man,
but actually a woman. It is a surprising realization, but I do not flinch
in facial expression or mannerism.

ME

Hi.

MATT

Hello.

ME

I have to say that you fooled me. I thought you were a man; in fact, I've been trying to build up the courage to ask you out since I sat down.

MATT

(smiles proudly)

ME

Is that real hair on your face?

MATT

No, it's fake. I glue it on.

ME

I'm Tom. Nice to meet you.

MATT

I'm Julie; most people call me Matt.

ME

I think it's great you came here looking like that. Next time you see me, please feel free to come sit with me at the bar.

MATT

(smiles)

Thank you. I'm so glad I can come here and be myself. Without this place there would be nowhere for people like me to go.

After a minute or two of conversation, we part. As I head to my car through the well-lit parking lot, I spot the bar owner, Barbara, and stop to talk to her. Barbara, who is in her early seventies, is known and loved by all for her toughness, support, acceptance of all, protection, and love of the gay scene.

BARBARA

(angrily)

Just chased away another couple who were making fun of my customers. Nobody makes fun of my customers. I run a clean and safe business here. No drugs, no bullying, no crime. Everyone is welcomed except the ignorant … and I told them just that.

ME

(shocked)
You went right up to them?

BARBARA

(proudly)
Yes, I did. And I also told them if they ever come back, I'd call the police, and off they went.

ME

(concerned)
Barbara, how are you feeling? I heard you've been sick.

BARBARA

I was just telling the guys last night that the tests came back, and I need to start taking it easy. The doctor's biggest concern is I stop smoking before I need oxygen.

ME

And what is your biggest concern?

BARBARA

(pausing for a minute and speaking sadly)
That my grandson doesn't have a profession. He needs to quit acting like he did in high school.

ME

(pausing)
Why doesn't he become a personal trainer? You told me he's been into bodybuilding since he was a teen. So he already knows the basics. And he's good with people.

BARBARA

What would Brian have to do to become a personal trainer?

ME

Last year they held a weekend course at the gym.
Brian will remember because he told me it disrupted
his workout schedule. At the end you got your PT
certificate. If that doesn't work, there are other options.

BARBARA

(pleased)

Would you talk to him? Just put a bug in his ear. It'll
sound better coming from you; he won't listen to me.

ME

Sure. He wants to go out to dinner next week, so I'll
be able to talk to him about it then. I think he likes me
because I told him he looks like the guys on the movie
cases we buy.

There is a tragic story surrounding Brian. When Brian was an infant, Brian and his parents were in a horrific car accident. The car was traveling at sixty miles an hour when a front tire blew, resulting in the car exiting the road and hitting a tree. In the years prior to mandatory seatbelt usage and sitting in the front seats, Barbara's son and daughter-in-law both died immediately upon the violent impact. Brian sat safely secured in his infant car seat behind his parents.

Barbara and her husband's world was shattered the day of the accident, as they lost their only child. In all of their grief, they decided to raise their infant grandson as their own. A couple of decades later, Brian grew into a near spitting image of his deceased father. Although Brian was an infant and couldn't possibly remember his parents or the accident, I think he projects a certain aura of longingness. So sad and tragic.

6 Ass To The House

Every neighborhood has one of them. Mine was fortunate to have two. I know I am not alone in using various techniques to get attention. Once I got in shape I wore Under Armour compression shirts that highlighted my muscular frame. Why not? I worked hard for it. People should notice me! And, for the right reasons, people should notice you too.

But when someone attracts unwanted attention by supposedly not wearing undergarments and carelessly but briskly displaying private parts while bending over doing yard work, that's grounds for a war! You could say my street was a war zone between Sheila and me.

As usual, Jack begins barking as I approached the fence.
                              ME
            (handing Jack a treat)
            Here you go, Jack.
Jack puts his front paws up on the fence and extends his head to grab the treat. I stand back for safety. Once Jack takes the treat in his mouth, he walks several feet away and eats it.
                              ME
            Ah, good puppy.
When he finishes, Jack resumes his spot by the fence—paws on the ground—and recommences attack mode. While returning home, I spot Sheila on the other end of her property. With several varieties of healthy plants and shrubs on her property, it seems Sheila is always doing yard work. Her green thumb is in contrast to my brown one. Sheila is standing bent at the waist, weeding in a sundress. Once

again I'd swear she isn't wearing any underwear or bra, confirming a comment Howard had recently made to me.

ME

(annoyed and yelling across the yard)

Ass to the house. Sheila, how many times have I told you? Ass to the house! You are the reason they put up the four-way stop.

Technically, if I counted the guy down the street who stood naked in his windows, my neighborhood had three of "us." He was eventually hauled off, or so I heard, so I don't count him. I truly hope that our (Sheila and my) competitive nature wasn't the impetus for his awful behavior. I'm going to ask Sheila which one of us she thinks gave him the stiffer competition. Oh, just for the record, I always wear undergarments, even under a bathing suit.

7 Don't Mix Brands

O nce I started working out at xCellFitness, I realized how different it was than my garage. Immediately, I learned proper technique by watching others. Sometimes a nice soul would stop me during my workout, claiming to correct my form "before I got hurt."

Most of the people I met were like me, gym nerds. Although many of us worked out or even trained, we were nowhere close to being considered "A-list" gym members. Very early in my gym membership, I met Victoria. She is one of the truly nicest and most beautiful human beings I know. Victoria, in her twenties, appears somewhat timid and nerdy, wearing glasses similar to the ones Gilda Radner wore in "The Nerds" sketches. Her compression clothing reveals that there isn't an ounce of fat on her.

Typically, early in the morning or after work, the personal trainers are at the gym with their clients. Sometimes a trainer trains multiple people at once in a group—as Megan often did. Tonight Megan trains her "girls."

In front of the xCellFitness children's playroom.
GYM MEMBER
(to crying child, Opal)
Honey, won't you please play in the kid's room so I can work out? You had fun the last time. Please.
VICTORIA
Girls, come here.
Victoria's young daughters appear from the playroom.
(to the little girl)

Hi. I'm Victoria and these are Jessica and Jesse. What is
your name?

OPAL

I am Opal.

VICTORIA

Opal, Jessica and Jesse would love to play with you.
They have all kinds of games and things to do in the
playroom. And if you need your father, he is just over
there. Would you like to play?

Opal shyly nods her head in agreement. The three kids go off into the
playroom.

GYM MEMBER

Thank you, Victoria.

In the free weights area, I am with Judy working out. I hear a trainer
talking to his client.

LEE

Never mix brands between your tops and bottoms.

Of course I recognize Mr. "Shape Up or Ship Out" from that first
night. Perhaps Lee is trying to tell me something since he was talking
loud enough for me to hear. And I am certainly guilty of brand
mismatching with my awful outfits.

ME

(to Judy)
Who is that?

JUDY

That's Megan's husband, Lee. He may play on the same
team you do.

ME

(disbelieving)
Hell, they say every great looking guy is gay … just look
at me.

JUDY

Shit, Megan just walked in. We'd better pick up the
pace.

ME

Why?

JUDY

She and her girls will hog the equipment.

ME

But we are already working out.

JUDY

Doesn't matter. People have left this gym because of her.
If she wants the equipment you are using, she will send
her girls over to use it during your break between sets.
Your one-minute break will turn out to be five minutes.
She intentionally targets you by having her girls follow
you around until it gets to a point where you can't even
finish your workout.

ME

Sounds like she should be the one to leave.

Judy and I are about to perform woodchops on the cable machine. If
you can envision the motion of swinging an ax to slice wood, you've
got a rough idea of the exercise. I go first. Judy observes my stance as
I prepare.

JUDY

No, Tom. You've got to stand with your feet apart. Let
me show you.

I step aside and Judy shows me the exercise, and I do it.

ME

How did you learn how to bodybuild? You make it all
look so effortless.

JUDY

The guys taught me.

ME

Looks like they taught you quite a bit.

JUDY

(smiling)
Oh, I taught them a thing or two.

Victoria appears on an adjacent machine.

JUDY

Tom, this is Victoria.

ME

Nice to meet you.

VICTORIA

Hi. You are new I've noticed. I used to be huge—Judy
remembers—and I lost some weight.

Victoria looks in the mirror, which displays a young woman without
an ounce of fat.

I've got a long way to go until I reach my goal.

Judy ignores the statement because she's heard it many times.

ME

(surprised)
What goal is that? Your weight at birth?

VICTORIA

(focusing on the mirror)
About another twenty pounds. I figure if I bump up
cardio an extra hour a day, I can lose it in no time.

My eyes widen, my mouth opens, and my head turns to one side and
slightly backward, as I am surprised by the statement.

ME

My God, the vultures would pass you by. I don't think
we're looking at the same person.

VICTORIA

I want to be beautiful like Megan, her girls, and the
women in the magazines.

Judy and I just look at each other in disbelief. Victoria is the gold
medalist. Megan couldn't even make tinfoil.

Thinking about what Lee said about mixing brands, I believe you've got
to look the part to play the role. I took the hint and within a few days I
purchased all new professional athletic attire and never again wore mixed
brands simultaneously.

8 Life Is about Love

One day a miracle happened at work. I was in disbelief as I read an email announcement stating our work area was being refurbished. Volunteers were being solicited to sit in temporary seating throughout our vast complex. It was clear this was going to be a long renovation and multiple temporary seating locations might be required.

Cynthia and I were overjoyed with this solution to our Elaine problem and immediately volunteered. We couldn't believe our good fortune. I didn't care if I had to personally walk one pencil at a time to my new desk while carrying Cynthia on my back. I was so ready. We requested, when possible, to be seated near each other in our new environment. Surely any area had to be better without Elaine's constant disruptions. During the year or so, we were probably moved three or four times and often, but not always, seated in the same area. Regardless of where we sat, we always managed to coordinate breaks and meals so we saw each other almost daily.

It is a beautiful day, so Cynthia and I decide to eat lunch outdoors. Despite our often cramped working conditions, the outdoor cafeteria seating is spaciously configured with an abundance of room between the solid wrought iron tables with matching heavy chairs. The outdoor dining area furniture and setting seem out of place in this corporate environment as though transported from a historical mansion. We sit under the large porch with beautiful blooming roses climbing on lattices. It is my favorite part of the entire vast complex. No one is sitting near us, enabling us to talk freely and openly.

ME

Thank you for being such a real person. In twenty years
of working at many places, this place is definitely the
worst. People make up their own reality! They blatantly
lie about their qualifications, their work, and about
their coworkers. There is little to no documentation on
anything, and nobody seems to know much or care.
Prior to meeting you, I thought I was the only one who
observed these things.

CYNTHIA

It's always those from the outside who can easily see
the issues. The key to working here is having low
expectations.

ME

It's more like having no expectations. How did Gene
ever become a manager? He has zero basic management
skills.

CYNTHIA

He's a club member. And I don't mean the HairClub
For Men!

ME

He's so out of touch, I think he only touches himself.
He couldn't direct traffic on a one-way street closed for
repairs.

CYNTHIA

It wasn't always like this. Before the first merger,
this was a great place to work—well managed with
experienced staff. You looked after the firm, they looked
after you. We were proud to be a part of it. Once the
mergers happened, it was like the clown car pulled up
and stayed. Now there's a whole fleet of them.

Cynthia leans into the table and softens her voice.

I was in a women's leadership event last week, and the
keynote female executive speaker said, "Well, my best

advice is to fake it until you make it." Can you believe that?

ME

Yes, I can. Twice I heard someone on the phone calling this place a "shit show." It's such a shame that generations of best practices and lessons learned are being thrown away just to increase the share price. Managers put their friends in positions for which they are not qualified. Everything is slapped together like a house built with toothpicks. Checklist mentality without regard for work quality or the long-term impact. This company is run like a Saturday morning pickup touch football game.

CYNTHIA

At this rate it will last just as long! Nowadays work has turned into arts and crafts to paint a rosy picture of project status to justify management's existence. I put more planning into Easter dinner than I see in the projects I participate in.

ME

And I bet your Easter dinner turns out wonderfully. You know, years ago I realized I would never climb the corporate ladder. I could simultaneously stand on my head, breathe fire out my nose, stop bullets between my toes—all while shooting fireworks out my ass—and I'd never be recognized. And I'm okay with that. I figure through investing I can still have a great retirement. As bright as I am, as hardworking as I am, as good as I am told my work is, I just don't belong in the social welfare club of corporate America.

CYNTHIA

I know. I had it hard being a woman in IT, but I bet you had it worse.

ME

Oh, I've been put through the wringer. Been called
a fag, promised promotions and other things only to
watch others get them who did little more than show
up to work. Once I believed the crap in the company
brochures about the open door policy, diversity, work
recognition, equal opportunity, and all that shit. Finally,
I realized it doesn't apply to everyone—just a select
few. I've learned that life, particularly work, is one
disappointment after another. It's how fast you recover
that counts.

CYNTHIA

Everyone has their own survival method. It's funny with
the ladies from the 1980s in technology. They seem to
fall into being whorish ...

Cynthia pushes out her chest, shows a little cleavage, rolls her tongue
around her mouth.

... or very submissive so as to not draw attention ...

Cynthia puts her hands up and raises her shoulders like she needs
someone to come to her aid.

... or they act like a man ...

Cynthia holds a pretend cigar in her mouth, while speaking in a deep
voice.

How about them Mets?
(voice returns to normal)
... or rude and obnoxious like the world revolves
around them.

ME

How have you persevered?

CYNTHIA

I was a poor single mother with kids to feed. I couldn't
screw around or screw up. I budgeted every cent. If I
had to work nights, weekends, or holidays, that's what

I did. And still do. My parents lovingly understood and babysat.

ME

I never had kids, so in that respect I guess I had it easy. I took the Lucille Ball approach to work: do any job that comes along because it means gaining experience. It was usually the tough stuff that nobody wants, appreciates, or recognizes. But I learned a lot. I never learned to bullshit, and I stayed clear of politics. I think politics is the work of the inexperienced.

CYNTHIA

My one regret is I never finished college. Maybe one day. It had better be soon because my memory is fading faster than my hair.

ME

Do you think it's the result of all that hair dye absorbed into your scalp?

CYNTHIA

It's more like age.

ME

But your life and work experience have far exceeded the value of a college education. I don't think it will help you in your career at this point. But what you did miss was living on campus and the thrill of having roommates.

CYNTHIA

I don't see myself as Rodney Dangerfield in *Back to School*.

ME

That was a great movie. Speaking of back to school, one of my former roommates turned out to be gay. He's in a great relationship with his partner, and they've been together for many years. I've slept over at their house, and I see the love and respect they have for each other.

That's what I want. Their relationship gives me hope that I can find one too.

CYNTHIA

What happens in your relationships?

ME

Most of the guys always need to go someplace or do something. (pausing sadly) I was never anyone's destination.

CYNTHIA

Just keep trying.

ME

Oh my God. I just remembered this. So my parents would send me food in college. I always told my roommates they could have whatever food they wanted, just don't finish anything. So one day I walk in, and my roommate informed me that he missed lunch and ate my cookies. Had I known back then he was gay, instead of eating my cookies, he could have been eating my nuts!

CYNTHIA

Would they have been salted or unsalted? (laughing)

ME

Dry roasted! You know, Cynthia, I worked extremely hard in college. I earned my grades; it didn't come naturally. But the most important lesson and, in many ways, the only lesson to learn is that life is about love. And love manifests itself in different ways like, "How are you?" and "I have missed you."

CYNTHIA

How would you classify "Fuck off?"

ME

The same way you would. You already understand and practice that lesson, so consider yourself college educated.

From our interactions, I began to see that Cynthia and I had several key character traits in common:

- Most importantly, Cynthia and I love to laugh. We laugh at ourselves, others, and the situations that life presents. If laughter is the best medicine, we frequently overdose. Through the good times and bad times, we just laugh!

- Both of us are very hardworking and honest individuals, who are probably greatly undervalued.

- We are both realists—meaning we state reality without being the center of it and are open to differing opinions.

- We both believe others have the right to act, behave, and live any way they want to as long as others aren't negatively impacted.

It drives me crazy when people rudely tell me, without being solicited, what they "would" or "would not" do in my a situation for which they have only a cursory knowledge. Or worse, they judge only to validate or justify their own actions, beliefs, or way of life. With this approach they are discounting others and missing out on understanding perspectives different from their own. Many people criticize others for not behaving as they would behave. Who says you set the standards for my behavior? Get over yourself.

Fortunately, Cynthia doesn't act that way, or we wouldn't be friends. I value the time I spend with Cynthia because of her insights, perspectives, and especially the humor.

9 Practice Makes Perfect

I was intimidated and insecure for a long time before I met enough gym members to guarantee at least one friendly face in the gym during my visits. I soon realized that other gym members were intimidated and insecure about people unlike themselves—specifically meaning me! I didn't know if the cause was human nature, gym demographics, or that some members felt afraid their hard-core gym would turn queer. But me, intimidating? Take it from me, I am one of the nicest individuals you'll ever meet!

Inside xCellFitness during the evening. I am shocked when Neal, a guy in his mid-to-late twenties and a high school graduate from a working-class family, walks up to me while I am on the treadmill.

NEAL

Hey man, quit staring at me. It creeps me out.

ME

Sorry, no clue what you're talking about. Do you think, subconsciously, you were hoping I was?

NEAL

Just cut it out.

Neal walks away.

VANESSA

I wouldn't waste my corneas on that loser.

ME

Actually, I was practicing using the mirrors to watch people. You've got to be prepared for the appearance of a hottie. It wasn't him I was looking at, per se. I would have looked at anyone in that challenging location. He just happened to be there. Besides, he couldn't have known I was looking at him. You know, I think Drew is onto something with this mirror stuff.

It took me a long time to perfect people watching using the mirrors. Through mirror angles and reflections, I eventually became skillful at observing people all over the gym. I wonder if anyone ever watched me? Probably not.

10 Sadness at the Celebration

I'll be the first one to admit that life is beautiful. But there are wake-up calls—those little and not so little reminders that we'd better not take life for granted. I don't know about you, but for me, one such wake-up call was John's celebration of life.

John was a gay man in the Pawtucket area who died of cancer. I did not know John well, but I knew his best friend, Trevor. The celebration was quite lovely, held at Equilibrium early in the evening during the bar's typically slow period. Pictures highlighting John's entire life were mounted on large cardboard displays placed on various bar tables.

I am viewing John's photos when Trevor joins me.

TREVOR

My old friend. It's great to see you. Thanks for coming.

ME

It's so sad about John. He was so funny. So young.

TREVOR

Just a year younger than us.

ME

I was thinking of dating him last year. It was wonderful
how you took care of him right up to the end.

TREVOR

Thank you. John and I go way back, and I am glad I
could help. And he was a great guy.

THOMAS M. CAESAR

ME

I didn't realize that cancer could take someone so
quickly.

TREVOR

I thought he'd pull through. I knew things were bad
when I'd hear music coming from his room late at
night. When he was scared, for strength he would play a
song called "Warrior."

ME

I don't know that song.

I love looking at pictures. Several photos stand out in my mind. My
heartstrings are tugged at the picture of John as a euphoric youngster,
struggling to hold back a lovable Labrador puppy intent on licking
his face. Then there is the picture of young John at the beach on
a raft, riding a wave and looking like he is freezing but having too
much fun to quit. Precious moments captured on film. As we view
the photographs, Trevor tells wonderful stories like the time John's
father thought the backyard shed had caught fire but instead found
John, Trevor, and several other neighborhood boys smoking behind it.

ME

My God ... the hair and the clothing. If this were my
celebration, the pictures would look exactly the same.
Except there wouldn't be any sports pictures. I retired at
the age of eight after I made a basket for the opposing
team and cried in front of everyone for five minutes.
You know, look at all the smiles in those Little League
and school pictures. This could be any of us. Back then,
you thought you'd live forever. Who'd wonder which
ones wouldn't make it in ten, twenty, forty, or fifty
years?

Trevor and I get teary.

I guess growing old is only for the lucky. Makes us
appreciate each other a little more.

We step aside from the cardboard pictorial displays to allow others to view them.

TREVOR

What's this I hear about you helping Brian become a personal trainer?

ME

Yes, Barbara had a concern that he didn't have a profession. So I suggested he become a personal trainer. I've had a few dinners with him. With each dinner I push him closer to it.

TREVOR

How is that going?

ME

The dinners or the suggestion?

TREVOR

Both.

ME

The dinners are painful. We don't have anything in common. He's never done anything or been anywhere. We only talk about the bar, the gym, and his grandmother. But I know Barbara is very appreciative of my efforts. After each dinner I report the progress. He's warming to the idea. At least now he isn't saying he can't do it. I figure if he doesn't agree to take the personal trainer course after two or three more dinners, I'll turn up the pressure by asking him to train me to see how easy it is. If I can pull this off, it will be his biggest personal accomplishment since his potty training!

TREVOR

Well, my friend, you are a nicer guy than the rest of us. The guys don't want anything to do with him ever since that beach trip. He called his grandfather to pick him up because he was frustrated that none of the women he

met believed he was straight, since he was traveling with
us guys. But he looked great in a bathing suit.

ME

I heard about that. I would be so embarrassed calling
for a ride when it's not an emergency.

TREVOR

He shouldn't have gone on the trip. Hey … how was
the cruise through the Panama Canal?

ME

It was excellent. On the actual day to transit the canal, I
was on deck, leaning against the railing overlooking the
bow of the ship at five o'clock in the morning. By the
time the sun rose, the deck behind me was packed three
deep. Since there were only twenty people under the age
of fifty, those around me were elderly.

As I was facing forward toward the bow of the ship, an
old tattooed tan hand holding a camera was thrust by
my left ear. I could tell by the hand that it belonged to a
much older man. Then I felt the grind of the old man's
hard-on against my ass. I did not turn around or cause
a scene.

I was impressed the old guy could still get a hard-on.
For the rest of the trip I wondered who, out of the two
thousand passengers, it was.

Trevor laughs and spots other people he knows.

TREVOR

Take care, my old friend. I'll talk to you later.

Trevor left me and I went back to viewing John's pictures. Pictures are windows into someone's life, and I feel that studying them is a great tribute to
the deceased. It took days for me to shake the feeling of impending death.
Quite sadly, John's relatives did not accept his sexual orientation, and not

one of them attended his celebration. John deserved better. Fortunately, it was well attended by the local gay and lesbian community. Here's to you, John.

11 Slow Progress

As regularly as the night turns into day, Jack got his treats—regardless of the weather. On rainy days, if he was outside, he'd come out from under a big bush.

Gradually, Jack stopped barking as I approached. I knew I had made progress. Jack is already waiting with paws high on the fence.

ME

Here you go, Jack.

As usual, I stand back for safety. Jack takes the treat in his mouth, leaves the fence, walks several feet away, and eats it.

Ah, good puppy.

When he finishes, Jack resumes his spot by the fence with his paws on the ground and looks at me. Wow, no barking as I depart. It appears to some degree Jack no longer considers me an intruder.

I remember the day clearly, because when Jack stopped barking at me, he stopped permanently. It also meant that my plan may actually work.

12 Good Meat

Barbara did so much for my community that helping her grandson choose a profession seemed like a small repayment. Our dinners were very challenging because Brian and I had little in common—very little. I couldn't fill the time talking about Loretta Lynn or country music, home projects, work issues, investments, or travel, since he lacked those experiences. Topics that Brian had mastered, such as sports, the military, and weapons, I knew nothing about. While some people may think Brian fits the "dumb jock" label, I never felt that way. Fortunately, I didn't let his lack of experience or his idiosyncrasies influence my opinion of his intelligence or good-naturedness. On the contrary, I thought he was smart.

Brian was very athletic, muscular, and model-like handsome. Brad Pitt would be envious and maybe even excited. Without any effort, he always drew great attention from both men and women. So no matter how challenging the meal got, at least I had eye candy to look at. I also need to point out I benefited from those meals too. As a single person, I didn't have to go out alone. Better yet, I didn't have to pay for a second meal just to have company.

One evening, inside a steakhouse. Brian and I are eating without speaking while laughter is heard from the surrounding tables. As with all bona fide gym rats, eating out provided a change of scenery but not a change of menu—we ate chicken breast, sweet potato, and broccoli, as always. The bread and butter went untouched. The beverage was water with lemon—no alcohol, soda, or iced tea.

ME
(breaking the silence)
I think Lee's a nice guy. He at least acknowledges me by
saying hi and not ignoring me like Megan.

BRIAN
(stops eating to answer)
Yeah, he's a good guy.

ME
Is Lee gay? Megan keeps making comments around me.

BRIAN
No, he's not gay. Sometimes trainers act interested in
guys so they will give them money to buy "the juice."
It's expensive.

I assumed "the juice" meant steroids and not Minute Maid. Finally,
after decades of practice, an attempt to deduce word meaning from
context may have actually worked.

ME
Have you thought more about being a personal trainer?

BRIAN
Man, I don't know about the personal trainer bit.

ME
Why not? You've been training yourself for years. People
like you, so why not train others and make money?

BRIAN
Think so?

ME
Yes. Just look around—no shortage of prospective
clients.

BRIAN
(looks at those seated in proximity)
I guess it can't hurt to look into it.

I was never a Boy Scout, but I pride myself on being prepared. I had
placed several pages of personal-trainer-related information printed
off the internet between the pages of a magazine for safekeeping.

Then I carried the magazine into the restaurant and put it next to me in the booth. Removing the personal trainer printed sheets from the magazine and holding them above the table, I start speaking.

ME

I printed this stuff out for you.

I point to the first page.

Here is a listing of local weekend personal trainer
courses with their dates and locations.

As I turn to the second page, our waitress comes to our table.

This page has websites that offer personal trainer courses
…

WAITRESS

How is everything?

BRIAN

Good.

WAITRESS

I'd like to apologize for the delay in receiving your food.
We are short staffed in the kitchen today.

ME

Any longer and I was going to suggest we go to the food
bank instead.

WAITRESS

Do you gentlemen belong to our rewards program,
Good Meat?

ME

I am a member but not in your program.

The waitress laughs at my comment, and once she leaves the table I resume reviewing the information I brought. Brian is very interested, tonight appears to be the breakthrough event. I couldn't be happier.

Warriors in our faction must remember when helping people beyond a one-time simple gesture, there are two factors that must be determined:

First you must define the scope of your involvement. The scope specifies what you will and won't do for someone, as well as identifies the signs(s) to you that your efforts are successful. Make sure your scope criteria(s) are realistic, sensible, and timely, especially if you alone have to plan and execute the help.

With Brian, the scope of my involvement is proposing that he become a personal trainer and providing him with a detailed path to make it a reality. That's it. My job is done. Brian is the one who must determine and execute all the tasks required for a successful reality including the registering, attending, studying, testing, and financing of his education. If he wants it bad enough, he will make it happen. As the warrior, my success is linked to the execution of my activities regardless of how Brian actually responds. As the old saying goes, "You can lead a horse to water, but you can't make him drink." The signal for success is the fact that I proposed, researched, collated, and presented him the path to becoming a personal trainer.

Never attempt to tackle situations requiring trained personnel unless you are qualified. For example, for someone with a substance abuse problem, success is to be clean. Most warriors would not be qualified to aid someone through drug withdrawal, so instead, the warrior's scope should be focused on the execution of smaller, but equally important subtasks such as organizing an intervention or encouraging someone to seek professional help. Consider contacting a professional to seek recommended techniques you may use to help the individual.

The second factor a warrior determines is when to stop helping someone. This is known as the "exit criterion." Since you can't help someone indefinitely, I highly recommend that you limit your involvement to a predetermined quantity (such as a time period, financial amount, or emotional strain) and some indication (perhaps an achievement or interest level) that the recipient is receptive.

I had two possible exit criteria with Brian's project, and I'd gladly accept whichever came first: either Brian selects a profession or four months pass. And during those four months, I will help him as long as I see he is making mental and/or physical movements toward any profession, not just the one I recommended.

13 Unintentional Influences

Tina and Rich were fun, and I loved being around them. Technically, they were old enough to be my parents, but they certainly didn't look or act like them.

I first met Tina and Rich when they bought Tina's parents' old mansion. It required a lot of renovation and maintenance. I was hired to cut their one-acre lawn back in my early teens. They paid well, and I enjoyed being around them, so I was always available for any chore needed. Through the years I did all sorts of jobs—yard work, shoveling snow, painting, staining, cleaning house, etc. One time, they locked themselves out of the house. Someone—not me—had the great idea that *I* should climb to the second-floor bathroom window and break in! I hope they've since put a key under a flowerpot like everyone else. I would say from my junior high school through high school years, I was over there at least once a week.

I often got invited to their family gatherings that included their friends. Naturally, I was thrilled to be included. As expected, they had fun family and friends, who treated an awkward teenager, like everyone else, with kindness and respect.

Just being around Tina and Rich I learned a great deal largely through observation. First, I saw how well they acted as a team: never in any circumstance was one of them the star and the other a supporting player. That is important because in any relationship, for any given characteristic, one person has the advantage. For example, one person is smarter, funnier, harder working, higher earning, holding a more prestigious job, and so on. In the end, a great relationship only results if it all nets to equal between the couple. And it did with Tina and Rich. Second, I saw how they planned and flawlessly executed (okay, sometimes flawed but with great humor) their projects. Don't get me wrong, Tina and Rich were very hands-on people, pulling up their sleeves to dig fence posts, stain ceilings, tear down walls, etc. They may have worn nice clothing and driven prestigious vehicles, which they would tell you they kept forever, but they weren't above doing any task. I may have been the paid help, but I also knew that either one or both of them could be working right beside me, and often one did. Third, the life pattern they had followed didn't escape my observation either. Having met in high school, they finished their education, married, became professionally (and probably financially) established, purchased and renovated their house, and then, in their midthirties, started having children.

Once I told Tina that she and Rich reminded me of Jonathan and Jennifer Hart on the popular television show *Hart to Hart*. They were attractive, fun, nice, funny, successful, and seemingly, at least to a teenager, wealthy. They were good, solid people of high moral and ethical character. Quite simply, they are the kind of people you want your kids to be, or the kind of person you want to be. Obviously, I never made it. If asked, Rich and Tina would say they never made it either. But they did.

Their big, old colonial house, dating back to the 1600s, holds a special spot in my heart. Just as when I was a teenager, I am still in awe when I see the home sitting so stately, as it has for hundreds of years, totally impervious to its surroundings. It blows my mind to think of all the people who have visited the house in its four hundred years of existence. If only its walls could talk. I continued to work at Tina's and Rich's house until I got my first real job after college. More importantly, they became my friends. Just being around them I absorbed and learned so much—much more than the money they paid me or any skill I learned doing their projects. Of course they have no way of knowing their positive contributions to my character during my formative teenage years. Next to my country music heroes, Rich and Tina had the largest influence on me.

Fast-forward twenty years. Tina and Rich were hosting Easter dinner at their house. The antique long, wooden dining room table and chairs perfectly matched the home's colonial character. Handwritten place cards identified our seats, and the overhead chandelier, consisting entirely of lit wax candles, illuminated the oversize silver cutlery, crystal, and fine china of the place settings. You'd think we were dining in Buckingham Palace.

For this holiday, Tina spared no expense or effort. The twenty-five guests were treated to a wonderful meal consisting of succulent roasted ham, airy homemade biscuits, creamy au gratin potatoes, sweet glazed carrots, and tender asparagus.

After dinner I found someone in their newly renovated, impressive kitchen washing dishes. I persuaded her to return to the dining room, and I resumed the dishwashing task. It was a pleasure and awe inspiring just to be in the kitchen.

The expansive kitchen had been thoughtfully reenvisioned into an elegant colonial-style gourmet kitchen. For decades the previous owner used the kitchen only to prepare food, but Tina and Rich turned the kitchen into both a first-rate culinary "studio" and a primary entertainment area. They completely gutted the room including its drop ceiling to expose a high ceiling with beautiful old beams. The huge old fireplace that had fallen into disrepair was rejuvenated into operational condition and became a focal point within the room. An adjacent storage room was annexed to become the kitchen's entertainment area. Admittedly, the luxury, high-end appliances and various culinary aids were lost on me, a Chef Boyardee–style cook. But fortunately, my dishwashing efforts don't require anything fancy or renovated—only a sink, dishcloth, soap, and dish towels.

There was a cloud over the joyous gathering. As beautiful as life is, it can also be cruel. Cancer, like all diseases, doesn't discriminate, and Tina has been battling it for years. But after decades of watching Tina and Rich battle all sorts of home renovation projects and contractors, I had no doubt they would battle and overcome the cancer all while telling wonderfully funny stories in the process—and for a long time they did.

Alone in the kitchen, I can hear talking and laughing from the other rooms. Infrequently, someone brings a dirty plate and sets it on the vast counter.

Tina walks into the kitchen.

TINA

Thank you so much for doing the dishes. I can't stand
long enough to do them.

ME

Tina, it's my pleasure. The host shouldn't be doing the
dishes—that's a job for a guest to show appreciation.
Dinner was terrific, especially the ham.

Tina takes a chair, puts it next to me, sits, and starts holding a dish
towel. She is sitting lower than the high countertop so I hand her
any wet, washed dishes that she can't reach. After she finishes drying
them, I put the dry dishes on the counter.

TINA

This year I had a lot of help, but I did the ham. The
secret to a good ham is to warm it up slowly. Most
people think because the ham is already cooked, they
can speed up the heating process.

ME

How are you feeling? I couldn't hear what you were
saying earlier.

TINA

I'm doing okay. I have a lot of tests this week and am
hoping for the best.

ME

Tina, I firmly believe that miracles happen every day. If
not today, maybe tomorrow. But a miracle won't happen
if you don't believe.

TINA

I need a miracle.

ME

(changing the topic)
You know, Tina, I have known you and Rich many
years and have seen a lot of wonderful changes to this

old house. But the best renovation is this kitchen. It is just beautiful.

TINA

Yes, it is. Rich gets the credit because most of the ideas were his.

Rich enters the room.

RICH

You won't believe this: we just got a new mower. I still remember the day you came to me with your hands up…

Rich demonstrates putting both hands up.

You said, "I refuse to use that old mower anymore."

ME

Well, hell, Rich, three of the wheels didn't turn. It was awful doing the lawn, especially the hilly part.

RICH

That was Grumps (Tina's father) for you, always buying the cheapest equipment.

TINA

Do you still remember that Fourth of July when we all gathered around that old tree to see the raccoon?

RICH

And after repeated directions, Grumps still couldn't see the raccoon?

We smile at that memory.

TINA

And you asked, "Do you still drive at night?"
(we laugh)
You are welcome here anytime.

14 True Beauty

For a long time, my closest xCellFitness friends were Drew, Judy, Vanessa, and Victoria. The longer I knew Victoria, the deeper I saw her beauty. To me, Victoria embodies the definition of beauty—that combination of physical and inner loveliness motivated by good-naturedness, selflessness, and compassion toward others.

However, Victoria didn't see it like that. Being a member of a hardcore gym with, quite frankly, beautiful people in tight clothing could be intimidating to anyone with self-esteem problems. I'd watched Victoria spend hours a day at the gym for months at a time. Despite frequent encouragement about how great she looked, she seemed to think that beauty consisted of only one characteristic—being bone thin.

Also, the longer I knew Victoria, the increasingly more concerned I became about her. I was very afraid Victoria's unhealthy body image would end with sad consequences, especially tragic with two young daughters who loved and needed her regardless of how she felt about herself.

Victoria and I are on the elliptical machines.

ME

Victoria, you train harder than Olympic athletes.
Which sport are you going out for? All of them? You are always here. How long have you been here today?

VICTORIA

A couple of hours.

ME

You look fantastic. You do realize I'm gay and have no

desire to get into your pants or blouse? I only wish I could wear them!

VICTORIA

I know.

ME

You are my major competition. Fortunately, I like you or you'd be injured by now! So when I say you look fine, I mean you look fine.

VICTORIA

I'm leaving soon.

ME

Good.

VICTORIA

Oh look, there's Zeke.

Zeke is the guy who wears the gray sweatpants.

I feel really bad for his son. On a child's birthday, the parents send in cupcakes for the class. Zeke's son's mother is in jail. Today was the boy's birthday, and my daughter told me he was embarrassed he didn't have any cupcakes. Had I known, I would have baked them.

ME

That little boy would have remembered your generosity for his entire life. Instead he will remember how embarrassed he was.

Since Victoria was brought up to be nice to people and do nice things for others, it is second nature to her. She doesn't understand that most people aren't brought up that way, so she couldn't know how rare her ingrained characteristics are.

I once told Victoria that I thought she'd find her forties to be the best time of her life. Hopefully, that's the time when we're over most of our childhood insecurities, have figured ourselves out, and realize life's roller coaster is going downhill. The problem was, at the rate she was going, I didn't think she'd make it into her thirties.

15 Happy New Year

Eventually, my almost daily gym visits and socializing started paying off. One of the "A-list" female gym members assumed I was invited to Pam's annual New Year's Eve party. When I told her I wasn't invited, she suggested I just show up because Pam "wouldn't mind." Generally, I don't attend a party where my invitation is absent or an afterthought. But I had heard about Pam's beautiful mansion and wanted to see it. After all, how many mansions do you know that have a private bridge leading up to them? Feeling uncharacteristically bold, I walked up to Pam and asked if I could attend. Graciously, she said she thought she had already invited me. We both knew she hadn't. Now that's class.

There is no question about it. Pam represented the upper 1 percent. Not only was Pam one of the more affluent gym members, but she also exuded class and sophistication. Whenever I'd see her in the gym, some good-looking guy aged anywhere from twenty-five to fifty was chatting with her. Okay, I was jealous. Her great figure, big hair, big boobs, and makeup went a long way to mask her sixty years of living. Of course, she was also very nice, witty, and approachable.

So with high hopes of seeing a beautiful mansion and an opportunity to "break into" the "A" group, I set off on New Year's Eve to Pam's house. Boy, did I see and learn a lot.

I find Pam in her enormous kitchen.

ME

(handing Pam a bottle of wine)
Happy New Year, Pam.

As though she needs glasses, Pam holds the bottle upward and outward to read the label. Although I am surprised by that action, I'm glad I purchased a respectable bottle of wine and not some cheap brand from the discount shelf, which I've been known to do.

PAM

Same to you.

ME

I see you have all the good-looking guys around you …
no doubt just like in high school.

Pam smiles.

ME

Pam, your house is beautiful. Can I take the self-guided tour?

PAM

Sure.

The tour through Pam's house is breathtaking including physically breathtaking; I feel like I am walking forever, as in a super Walmart. The house is a testament to her success in the business world. Each room—and there certainly are plenty of them—seems like a magazine feature. In her office, there is a lifetime of pictures on the tables. I spot one of Pam with President Obama. Impressive.

Surely Pam used a professional or perhaps an entire team to decorate her immense house. Somehow I don't think her furniture arrived in boxes that required assembly with cryptic, poorly printed instructions and a plastic bag full of hardware like my furniture did. If she didn't have an army to help her decorate the interior, she most certainly needs an army to clean it.

Janice had told me that the master bathroom was "unbelievable," so it was with great anticipation that I went to see it. I knew I found it when inside the master bedroom I spot two large pocket doors. Upon opening the doors and turning on the lights, the first thing that strikes me is the lights reflecting on the highly polished white Carrara-marble-tiled floors and walls. I feel like I've entered a cloud.

It takes a full minute to comprehend the full luxuriousness and beauty of the huge bathroom as I stand and survey the room. To the left of the entry are double sinks sitting atop a long white marble vanity. In the back left corner is a small room containing a toilet and bidet. To the right of the toilet room is a door that I did not open; I don't know if it leads to a hallway, a sauna, a laundry room, a wardrobe room, or some combination thereof.

Next along the rear wall and spanning approximately ten feet is the shower "room." It's practically a car wash for the human body. Through the clear, long glass front wall, I see a bench and the controls for the multiple shower heads surrounding marble walls and ceilings. I am amazed at how shiny and clean the glass wall looks—as if just installed or is perhaps seldom used.

In the right rear corner is the sunken bathtub set against mirrored walls and ceiling. In all fairness, the word "tub" is an understatement. It is the size of a very small and shallow pool. I'm surprised there isn't a lifeguard stand. I can't imagine how much water or time it takes to fill it.

Oddly and very perplexing, a seating area is across from the tub in the adjacent corner. Two beautiful gray leather wingback chairs separated by a white marble end table face the right corner where a flat-screen TV is suspended from the corner wall. I can't help but notice the full-size bar cabinet and compact refrigerator along the wall shared by the master bedroom.

Finally, between the refrigerator and the right entry pocket door is a wardrobe followed by a long white marble vanity makeup area with its single chair and various magnification mirrors suspended from the wall.

Wow.

I introduce myself to the people I passed on my self-guided tour, but I also note that people gathered throughout Pam's beautiful house segregated according to their affiliation to Pam (such as relatives, friends, neighbors, professional affiliates, and employees). Quite surprisingly they did not seem to intermix with the other groups except in the kitchen and dining rooms, where the food and liquor are placed.

At end of the tour, I stop back in the dining room to get food. The beautiful dining room features expensive catered food nicely displayed on a huge table. There is enough variety to satisfy any diet or ruin one.

The food is arranged in tiers on the dining table. The topmost tier is dedicated to beautiful large poinsettia plants with their pots wrapped in red and gold foil. The lower two tiers are dedicated to food. As I walk alongside the table, the appetizers appear first. I spot mini crab cakes, stuffed mushrooms, mini quiche, mini meatballs, shrimp cocktail, fresh fruit filling a carved watermelon, and a variety of cheese and crackers.

The rolls and butter are next, followed by the salad. Big bowls of iceberg and romaine lettuce are surrounded by smaller bowls of salad condiments like shredded carrots, celery, grape tomatoes, onions, cucumbers, chickpeas, broccoli, peppers, cheddar cheese, bacon bits, dried cranberries, beets, and cauliflower. The salad area concludes with a variety of salad dressings.

The main course follows: carved roast beef, baked fish, and lasagna along with appropriate condiments.

For vegetables, there are mashed potatoes, macaroni and cheese, rice pilaf, and corn.

With respect to the bodybuilders, Pam dedicates a whole section just for us consisting of chicken breast, asparagus, sweet potatoes, and broccoli.

Lastly are the desserts: chocolate cake, white velvet cake, mini cheesecakes, mini French silk pies, fruit and chocolate tarts, and finally an assortment of cookies.

I must admit I've been to weddings with a lot less food. I don't recall seeing any catering staff during the event, however, knowing Pam's generosity, she probably invited the catering staff to bring a date and celebrate the New Year at her party. Although the food was excellent and plentiful, had it been me, I would have served a variety of Stouffer's party-size entrees and every thirty minutes checked for empty tin pans to throw away.

As I am getting food, a rather large man whom I don't know starts talking to me. He is about to exit the dining room.

PAM'S GUEST

(extending his two plates of cheeses, cookies, and rich desserts to show me)

They say you are what you eat!

ME

(smiling)

I love fruit, that's probably why I became one.

I bite my tongue to stop myself from suggesting that he spread some butter on his thighs to guard against the postdigestion chafing that I anticipated would occur.

Back in Pam's enormous kitchen.

ME

Pam, your house is phenomenal. You could live in your
bathroom. I was going to make a comment about your
drapes matching the carpet, but I see you don't have any
curtains anywhere.

PAM

No, not a one.

ME

I bet the neighbor boys lurk in your bushes.

By then Sharon from the gym spots me and joins us.
She has a plate of chicken breast and broccoli.

SHARON

Hi. Tom, glad you could make it. We're all over here.

Somehow I had missed them on the house tour. I follow Sharon to
the rest of the group.

In Pam's study.

ME

(to group)
Hi.

Megan gives me a half smile. At least I got that. The others barely
notice me. I go over and stand next to Lee since he would say hello
to me at the gym. Lee is noticeably uncomfortable and moves to the
other side of the room by himself. I interrupt the other guys and
shake their hands.

ME

So what got you guys into bodybuilding?

I start eating while they talk.

KEITH

It was part of high school wrestling, and I just
continued it.

TROY

Junior school was a rough time for me. I got picked

on, and my parents thought bodybuilding was a way to become more manly. After a while, nobody ever messed with me again.

TED
I was just a shy, timid, skinny kid without friends.
My father thought working out would build my self-confidence. At first I worked with him in our basement. When I outgrew that, I joined a gym and found other guys my age, and we'd work out together.

I am shocked and speechless at these Adonises' revelations when Sharon speaks up.

SHARON
How about a toast for the New Year?
Everyone raises a glass.

Through the night I observe the non-bodybuilders had plates containing large portions of unhealthy food and lots of alcohol. The bodybuilders were eating small portions of high-protein food and consuming little alcohol.

At one o'clock in the morning, it was time to leave the party. As I left, I didn't see any neighborhood boys lurking in the bushes.

For a long time, I was bothered by the guys' revelations about what drew them into bodybuilding. These guys are now Adonises who have the world on a string. Who'd have thought they had such troubled pasts? I am amazed they admitted their stories to me. Eventually, I saw a pattern where those who got into the sport for adverse reasons only changed their bodies. Mentally, they hadn't overcome the childhood issues that initially plagued them. When you're in your teens that may be fine, but in your late twenties and thirties, it's time to overcome it.

I began to realize that it was different for me when I was growing up. I didn't feel the need conform to anything. I knew those who made fun of me and others were wrong, and the only change I made was to avoid those kinds of people and not be like them. I'm still that way today. People remedy the same situation differently, so, for some of my gym associates, the solution was to lift weights to make them feel secure with themselves. I wonder what I'd be like today if that was the route I had taken in my teens.

I enjoyed Pam's New Year's Eve party. It was the only time I went to Pam's beautiful house. I never pressed for another invitation. I did my best to mingle among the various disparate groups and found most everyone to be very sociable and outgoing. If nothing else, my attending the party gave the guys a reason to acknowledge me in the gym.

16 Trouble in Paradise

Vanessa comes out of the xCellFitness locker room laughing and shaking her head. As she approaches the treadmill next to me, she explains.

> VANESSA
> (matter-of-factly)
> Some lady was peeing, and a wet ceiling tile followed by
> a little liquid fell on her.

> ME
> What color was the liquid?

> VANESSA
> It was clear, thank God. Incredible.

Vanessa and I see a young girl hanging a collage of Megan's show pictures within a single frame by the round table.

> ME
> Why are they hanging that up? Who wants to see that?

> VANESSA
> Just one of her girls brownnosing her.

> ME
> Well, if my picture were hung up, it would be stolen
> and used as a sexual aid.

> VANESSA
> Never happen with hers. Target practice is more likely.
> Did you check out the front counter? There's a framed
> letter from someone claiming Megan is a wonderful
> person.

                    ME
You've got to be kidding.
                  VANESSA
I heard she didn't do so well in her last show. Guess the
judges didn't like her blow jobs.
                    ME
You serious?
                  VANESSA
That's the rumor. I believe it.
                    ME
Well, some other fag can teach her how to give a good
blow job. I'm not.

Surprisingly, Megan's pictures stayed on the wall for several years and
served as a reminder of that conversation. Not surprisingly, the framed
letter didn't stay long on the front counter, perhaps its author recanted his
statements!

17 "You Ain't Woman Enough"

To me, the New Year is a reminder to start cleaning the house for my annual party in mid-January. I host the party on the Sunday of MLK weekend, which gives me the Saturday to prepare and the Monday off to clean up. I begin each year by showing my appreciation to the local loved ones in my life, and I take great pride in doing so.

Since my house is small, I can have no more than ten or twelve. With only two rooms, everybody is forced to mingle. The only requirements I have is that everyone must be polite and respectful toward others and that nobody brings any food to the party.

I like to think of it as a first-class operation on a budget airline! I refuse to use those cheap paper plates (you know them—they require five plates for any strength), plastic utensils (they bend holding the food), and paper cups. Instead, I insist on using ceramic plates, metal flatware, and glasses or crystal. I do all the cooking myself, although in these later years that has changed. It's all self-serve, including the alcohol. Over the years I've learned how to make the event simple, since I do all of the effort. I've got the planning and execution down perfectly. Perfectly to the point where I can actually socialize and enjoy my own party.

Although many people should be invited, I like keeping the guests to a minimum. Personally, I think the small group intimacy is part of the success. You know it's a good party when the guests start soliciting invitations three months beforehand and return every year. The success of the party makes it difficult to invite newer individuals until someone moves out of the area or they tick me off enough to not be invited back. Why, it took almost ten years for spots to open to include two of my favorite local friends, George and Annette.

Originally the first floor of my house consisted of a full-length living room on one side, and the other side split into equally sized rooms for the kitchen and dining room. The stairs and closet separate the two sections. Several years after I moved in, I removed the wall between the kitchen and dining room thus creating a large kitchen, relatively speaking. Fortunately, there is room in the kitchen for a small seating area with a television in addition to a kitchen table.

The party set-up is always the same. All of the food and liquor are arranged on five folding tables in a basic *U* shape. In the rear of my house is a short walkway between the living room and kitchen, the first table is placed with dishes, flatware, and napkins. Turning into the rear of the kitchen, three additional tables are placed along the front to back spanning the kitchen wall. Tables two and three are dedicated to the food while table four consists of glasses, ice, and nonalcoholic beverages. The final table, number five, is against the front door in the small foyer between the kitchen and living room. It has all the alcohol, mixers, condiments (such as lemons, limes, and olives), and bartender accessories. Consequently, the front door is unusable forcing people to use the back door.

Inside my house.

HOWARD

This ham is delicious. Always great food in your house.

ME

Thank you. My friend Tina taught me how to prepare ham. Yep, nothing like good meat in the mouth!

SHEILA

You are crazy to cook all this food.

ME

I know.

CYNTHIA

Just serve Chinese food. Everyone loves it, and it's very inexpensive.

There is a faint knocking sound.

CYNTHIA

I think someone is knocking at the front door.

I pause to listen.

ME

Shit. Everyone knows with me to use the back door.
(smiling)

With the front door blocked by the alcohol table, I am forced to
signal to my guest through the front door window blinds to use the
back door. Unlike my perfected offensive figure gestures, I have a
difficult time communicating a clear gesture to inform my guests to
walk around to the back door. Meanwhile, I can hear my kitchen
guests talking:

HOWARD

How's Jack doing?

SHEILA

He's getting to be an old man with old man problems.
All things considered he's doing well.

CYNTHIA

Is Jack your father?

SHEILA

That's another old man! Jack is my dog, an Akita.

CYNTHIA

Those are very protective dogs. I bet he'd take your hand
off in a heartbeat.

SHEILA

Jack would. Tom is afraid of Jack. He's trying to get Jack
to warm up to him by giving him dog treats. I think
they're both starting to warm to each other.

Vanessa and Judy enter my house through the back kitchen door.
Immediately, like a moth to a flame Howard's eyes fixate on Judy's
large breasts.

ME

Let me introduce you. This is Judy and Vanessa from

the gym. Both Howard and Sheila are my neighbors.
Cynthia is the friend from work who keeps me sane.
Everyone is nice and fun, or they wouldn't be here.

HOWARD

(to Judy)

Maybe I should join your gym. Where is it?

JUDY

Up the Pike near Petey's.

HOWARD

That's a bad area.

CYNTHIA

And getting worse. I've told Tom repeatedly to stay clear
of that area.

ME

There are bad areas everywhere. Besides, it's close and
there are some nice people there … like these two.

CYNTHIA

(sternly)

There are nice people in better areas.

VANESSA

Can you show us around your house?

ME

Sure.

I have given the home tour many times, so it's well rehearsed. I point
to the picture on the kitchen wall.

This was my grandfather's house. He died in 1998, and
my mother inherited the house. She had such a hard
time with his death and settling the estate, I decided
to buy the house to make it easy on her. I didn't want
the house or to live here. So I was basically stuck with
a house from 1975 with avocado-green appliances
and rotary dial phones. It's been a huge money pit,
everything needed replacing or upgrading. There has
been little joy in homeownership.

As Vanessa, Judy, and I climb the stairs to continue on the tour, my kitchen guests seize the opportunity to talk about me. Unbeknownst to my company, the thin walls and floors in my house do little to mask their conversations, and we can hear them.

HOWARD

You've got to wonder about someone who has pictures of himself in every room.

CYNTHIA

I think that's his attempt at art.

HOWARD

Have you noticed the curtains? He's been almost all over the world and uses sheets for curtains.

SHEILA

These aren't sheets. They were too expensive. He used tablecloths.

HOWARD

I wonder how many years these will be up?

SHEILA

Don't let Tom hear you say that. He'll make it permanent out of spite. The homeowner association president told his parents it was disgraceful that Tom printed his house numbers on a sheet of paper and taped it to the front door. Five years later he has made no attempt to replace it with the house numbers he already bought.

CYNTHIA

The peculiar thing about Tom is he seldom spends two cents on himself except to travel. Instead, he'll waste time and money on people who are only interested in him for his generosity. I get on him all the time about it. He should be living much better than he does. Did you know he hangs his wash in the basement to dry? Who does that?

SHEILA

I'm surprised he doesn't wash his clothes on a rock by
the river.

HOWARD

He probably would if you weren't already there.

...

Surprisingly, everyone loves the karaoke and by the time Lee and
Megan arrive, most of my guests are participating in it. I am deeply
immersed in the full catering duties of replenishing near-empty
serving trays and gathering and washing plates, flatware, and glasses
for immediate reuse. Their arrival could not have been worse. I
manage to introduce them to everyone and leave them to socialize
with the other guests, including the two from the gym. Sadly,
they don't mingle with my other guests. Perhaps they appear too
intimidating or they are used to people making a fuss over them,
which is unlikely to occur in my house. In such a small house, I didn't
think it was possible for two people to isolate themselves, but that's
how it looks. Between catering duties, I sit with them when possible,
but it is awkward because it appears I am ignoring my other guests.

George enters the kitchen and finds me seated with Megan and Lee.
From the living room karaoke is filling my house with surprisingly
impressive singing by my friends Jon and Mike dueting on the classic
Tanya Tucker favorite "Delta Dawn."

GEORGE

Annette says she will sing "You Ain't Woman Enough"
with you. Will you do it this year?

ME

(nodding head affirmatively)

Several years ago I rewrote parts of Loretta Lynn's classic song "You
Ain't Woman Enough (To Take My Man)." And I gave it a huge twist.

I need to get my lyrics. I think they are in a drawer
in the powder room. Will the Back Door Boys be
performing tonight?

GEORGE

I don't know, maybe later. Can't we change our name? I don't like the name Back Door Boys.

ME

How about the Butt Blasters? (Butt Blaster is the name of a machine at the gym.)

CYNTHIA

(from across the kitchen)

With Tom involved, it should be Blasted Butt.

ME

Thanks, Queen LaQueefa.

Everyone gathers in the living room except for Lee and Megan, who remain in the kitchen. Annette and I are standing with microphones in our hands. Additionally, I have a napkin with my revised song lyrics in my other hand. As the karaoke music version of Loretta Lynn's "You Ain't Woman Enough (To Take My Man)" starts, I study my revised lyrics while Annette starts singing.

ANNETTE

You've come to tell me something you say I ought to know
That he don't love me anymore and I'll have to let him go
You say you're gonna take him, oh, but I don't think you can
Cause you ain't woman enough to take my man
Women like you they're a dime a dozen, you can buy 'em anywhere
For you to get him, I'd have to move over and I'm gonna stand right here
It'll be over my dead body, so get out while you can
Cause you ain't woman enough to take my man

Musical interlude between verses.

ME

Singing my revised second verse and chorus lyrics:

Sometimes a man goes lookin' to fulfill his needs

While he may be married to you, he keeps comin' back to
me
He's getting ready to leave you, listen and understand
You ain't woman enough to keep your man
Women like you cry tears by the dozen, I see it everywhere
You can't keep him so move on over and get on out of here
Yeah, I see your sagging body, listen and understand
You ain't woman enough to keep your man
No, you ain't woman enough to keep your man

Applause and laughter from the partygoers. The revised lyrics always make everyone laugh. Originally, it was meant as a one-time duet at my party, but it gets requested every year. And with me, a male, singing the revised second verse, every year it is a party highlight.

I felt bad for Lee and Megan. They didn't blend well with the other guests and probably didn't have any fun—I knew I wasn't having fun, and I was relieved when they left. Once they left, I had a great time. The party lasted well into the night. Judging from the guest departure comments, this was another successful party. More importantly, I am delighted to have such wonderful people in my life.

18 Nothing at All

Victoria and I are on adjacent treadmills.

                    VICTORIA
        Don't think I'm crazy, but I've decided to train one or
        two days a week with Megan. I've gained a little weight,
        and I know working with her I'll lose it.

I was delighted that Victoria had gained a little weight and was
no longer just skin and bone. However, I was very disappointed
that she'd want to train with Megan. Victoria had complained that
Megan's girls were talking about her in the locker room. Putting
Victoria into that mix was like putting a pat of butter into a hot
frying pan.

                      ME
        (sternly)
        The only weight you've gained is from letting your
        hair grow longer. And that's measured in ounces, not
        pounds.

I did not say anything more to Victoria about it.

Privately I was upset with Megan for her insensitive public comments
about Lee. She had been telling stories for weeks, if not months,
that—regardless of whether true or not—would be upsetting to a
highly private person like Lee. I know I was upset enough for both
me and Lee.

After finishing cardio and saying goodnight to Victoria, I spotted
Lee's best friend Keith at the round table sitting by himself.

On my way out I stop to talk to Keith.

ME

I need to talk to you. You're Lee's closest friend, and I
know you respect him and want what's best for him.
None of this is any of my business. But Megan's going
around staying stuff about Lee. If she's telling me, I can
bet she's telling other people. She's saying stuff like: "Lee
called the gay help line thirty times from *my* cell phone.
He needs to come out."

KEITH

Yeah, I know.

ME

If she is trying to out him, that's not helping him. Or
maybe she's just bitter about the pending divorce and
wants to embarrass him. Either way, it's unacceptable.
I heard he lives in his parents' basement and has asked
Megan to help him with his bills. So I guess he doesn't
have much. The one thing he does have is this gym, and
I know he enjoys it. She needs to change her approach.
I can't help him; he wants no part of me.

KEITH

Hopefully, the worst is over.

Helping others can be a tricky endeavor. I'm no doctor or therapist, but I
realize that most people, when they get involved, base their efforts on their
own experience, resources, and limitations with little thought or reflection
for the consequences or the wishes, needs, and interpretation of the one
being helped. I guess nobody wants to put themselves *in someone else's shoes*.
So be mindful to (1) remember that you can't control a person's response
to your actions, (2) try to anticipate how your actions may be perceived by
both the person you are helping and others, and (3) keep someone's per-

sonal and confidential information private. Even with the best intentions, the warrior's actions should never intensify an already bad situation of the one being helped.

Sometimes doing nothing to help someone is preferred over actions that may cause more damage (such as physical, mental, financial, or reputational) to the one being helped. After all, are you truly helping someone (being altruistic) or just helping yourself feel better (being self-indulgent)?

I'd like to think that Megan was trying to help Lee rather than embarrass him. However, sharing someone's confidential information isn't acceptable. In this case, Megan should do nothing. Sometimes less is best.

19 What's the World Coming To?

After a while, the gym Adonises opened up to me. I credit three things for breaking down the barriers with the bodybuilders: First, I was at the gym five to seven days a week. Second, I hung out with Judy, whom the guys had trained and accepted. Third, I met the guys at Pam's New Year's Eve party. Then one night I had a surprising conversation that really put things into perspective.

Peter and I are doing cardio on adjacent treadmills.

PETER

My daughter went to prom. I picked out her dress because she doesn't have any fashion sense.

ME

(shocked)

Really?

Peter continues to talk while he stops exercising to look for a picture on his phone. I scan Peter's workout clothes and realize his sneakers are coordinated with his outfit.

PETER

We went to the mall—just the two of us. Thirty minutes later, we were done. I picked out a beautiful black and gold dress. We got black shoes, gold earrings, and red lipstick. I made her an appointment to get her hair done.

Peter shows me the picture on his phone.

ME

(very surprised)

Wow. Beautiful. Are you sure you aren't gay—maybe
just a little?

PETER

Positive.

ME

Don't ruin the fantasy.

PETER

She couldn't have looked more beautiful, and she had a
great time.

ME

Have you started listening to Judy Garland yet?

I thought it was great that Peter was actively involved with his daughter's
prom, and he did a great job with the selections. Something tells me if Peter
had a gay son, he would be his son's biggest fan and help him dress in drag.
Not only did I have competition from the gym's busty bitches, but now
the straight guys were invading my home turf in the beauty and fashion
arena. What's the world coming to? Fortunately, I didn't feel threatened.
Even though my space may have been invaded, I had no plans to invade
anyone else's space. I refuse, among other things, to personally perform car
maintenance such as changing my own motor oil or rotating my tires!

The more I got to know the guys, the more I realized the bar and gym
people have many things in common, mainly wanting to be accepted and
the love of laughter. Both groups could be friends if only each side would
just drop their walls and preconceived notions. I had noticed a big difference in the two groups, though: *some people go to the bar to be themselves,
while some people go to the gym to hide themselves.* Intriguing.

20 Just This One Last Time

Very early on Sheila and I realized we share an unfortunate common trait—poor sleep. I don't know the cause of Sheila's problem, but I suspect mine is heredity. As a kid I vividly recall both my grandfather and his sister talking about their sleeping challenges, and I never thought that I would grow up to have the same ones. For me, if I'm awake during the night, my mind starts up and won't stop. Consequently, a night of good sleep is a rare event and I am extremely annoyed if anything or anyone disrupts me during it.

Through the years Sheila and I have tried many different sleeping solutions du jour, and often discuss their results. Personally, I find the best solution is to exhaust myself through exercise if my exercising does not result in any body aches that awaken me during the night.

I started joining Sheila on her frequent walks with Jack. I always put a dog treat in my pocket and would give it to Jack at the end of the walk. Although Jack no longer barked at me and was used to me, I was still very afraid of him. Generally, Jack stayed on the curb side of Sheila. Both Sheila and I carried water bottles. Mine was often filled with an adult beverage.

One oppressively hot and humid evening when every step is a major effort.

SHEILA
He smells the treat. Have you noticed he barks at you when he sees you across the street?

ME

Yes, and he also barks if there are strangers around my property.

SHEILA

My hair is awful in this humidity. Don't think I can make it a long walk. Poor Jack must be suffering too. You can pet him; he won't bite.

ME

I'm still afraid to.

SHEILA

You'll be fine. He's a very loving and protective dog. Yesterday I put up Beware of Dog signs on the fence. I saw a little girl go over to the fence while Jack was outside. Surprisingly, Jack did not bother with her, but I can't take that chance ... Are you sleeping better?

ME

No. I get about two hours of sleep. Most nights I just lie in bed thinking. What I can't understand is why Megan says stuff about Lee being gay in front of me. He never corrects her, not once. Is she trying to determine if I would date him? Is she hoping I would ask him out? Is this some sort of game they are playing, and I am just a pawn? Should I inform her that it isn't acceptable to publicly out someone? I just can't keep going on like this.

SHEILA

I thought that prescription was working.

ME

It did for three nights. Now it's useless.

SHEILA

Tom, please go to another gym. These two are not nice people.

ME

You don't even know them.

SHEILA

No, but I know you. I can see what they are doing to you.

ME

You could argue I'm doing this to myself.

SHEILA

They know exactly what they are doing. At least check out my gym. They're running a special.

ME

I already checked into it. I heard the locker room is full of old, naked men.

SHEILA

(laughing)

And that isn't an incentive?

Maybe you can help me. I just don't know what to do. My sister wants me to visit next month. She's going to be in a musical, but she's arguing with the director. If she gets the part, I will just be sitting around with her husband while she's in rehearsal. I can sit here or get things done around my house. My brother wants me to visit him in Texas. Maybe I'll do that instead. I don't know; it's just crazy. Maybe Will can watch Jack. Then there's Daddy. I am so concerned that he's still running that business by himself at his age. Maybe Howard can get my mail and paper.

ME

(interrupting)

Is this story going to be long? I took melatonin.

SHEILA

Stop it. I can't sleep either. I'm going to start taking Benadryl. Have you tried it?

ME

No. Just let me know what you need me to do around your house if you go away.

SHEILA

Speaking of Howard, I need to call him. There's a bloom
on my clematis.

ME

Don't worry. I hear there's medication that'll clear it
right up.

Sheila hated my clematis comment. I thought it was a riot and still do.
Through the years I told it many times until I could tell it was getting on
her nerves. A few years ago I promised I wouldn't tell it again. Okay, just
this one last time, I promise.

All of the stories Megan was spreading about Lee being gay had a big
adverse impact on me. I'd lose sleep—a lot of sleep—nightly. I can't begin
to estimate how much sleep I lost during that time. Cynthia and Sheila
went through it with me, so they could provide the best estimate. The
same pattern would occur nightly: First I'd be angry at how rude and insensitive Megan's new comments about Lee were. Then I'd wonder if there
was any truth to them and I'd be up at night excited at the thought that
an Adonis could be interested in me. In my mind I'd replay Megan's comments repeatedly. I questioned why she made the comments, why he never
corrected her when he was present, and why he never asked me out. Every
night, night after night. Then, reality would set in and I'd conclude there
was something wrong with me.

Looking back, I am amazed that, in my overtired state, I didn't have
some sort of car accident, injury, or health issue.

21 Heard It through the Grapevine

I always had one or both ears tuned into the gossip grapevine going all the way back to my elementary school days. Somehow, maybe because of my personable personality or the perception that I am trustworthy, I was a human tabloid in every environment in which I resided. I'm not saying I believed it all; I just knew it all. And like a good paper towel, I absorbed it all. It was fun hearing stuff about other people. Fun, that is, until I started hearing grossly or totally inaccurate stories about me. But then I heard something about Lee that piqued my interest.

Inside my home office. Cynthia and I are at my desktop computer. I am seated in a chair at the computer; Cynthia is standing next to me.

ME

Some of the guys at the gym said Lee was on a gay site.
I think I found him. Do you want to see?

CYNTHIA

Look, they are pulling your leg. You have been one big
joke to them for their amusement.

Realizing that Cynthia has never seen Lee, I searched the internet for Lee's bodybuilding competition pictures.

ME

(clicking away on my desktop computer)
I found some posing pictures on a bodybuilding website
for comparison. Here, look at these pictures of Lee.

CYNTHIA

Wow, I can see why you can't sleep at night. He is gorgeous.

ME

Now onto Manhunt.

CYNTHIA

Is that a gay website? Is there a Cunthunt site for women?

ME

Here you go. I'm not a fan of headless naked pictures.

CYNTHIA

Wow … look, this must be him.

Cynthia points to the screen.

I can see a trophy in the background!

I tilt my head to view the object Cynthia is pointing to. I hadn't observed it before.

ME

(surprised)

Notice Lee in the show competition pictures and the person on the gay site have the same frame, same skin color, no tattoos? I've heard Lee lives in his parents' basement. Don't those windows look like cellar windows?

CYNTHIA

I think you're right. Have you contacted him?

ME

Yes, several times we were supposed to meet. Each time he canceled at the last minute. Never once did he unlock his face pictures.

CYNTHIA

Guess he's not ready.

ME

You can't be gay unless you have someone to be gay with.

CYNTHIA

Come on, let's eat. I know how you get when you're hungry. I can't deal with you being hungry and horny.

22 Alone In The Nest

I was a terribly shy child who was petrified of separation from my parents, being in new environments, and meeting strangers. I loved the safety and security of my bedroom. The shyness extended through my high school years. Every morning for four years I would stop at a friend's house and "pick her up" on my walk to the high school. Ostensibly I stopped because it was on my way. The fact is, every morning I was so nervous about facing school that I needed her companionship; I found her carefree attitude greatly calmed me. Eventually some of her field hockey friends would join us, and there would be a small group walking to school. Recently I've learned a neighbor recalled how "silly Tom looked walking with a bunch of girls." Silly or not, it was a great cure that helped contribute to my high school success. It should come to no surprise that during the first days of my college freshman year, I stayed in my dorm room listening to country music, too scared to attend any of the meet-and-greet sessions.

Most people, whether they knew me back then or know me now, would find that very hard to believe. Of course, those same individuals also laugh at my claims of being an international male sex symbol. Oh well. Eventually, I learned how to act my way out of being shy in public, but I never got over it. As imbecilic as it is, even decades later, shyness will still strike. So I recognize and always appreciate when people go out of their way to help others, especially me, be comfortable and fit in. For a long time, the totally foreign gym world, where I didn't have much in common with others, was a terrifying place. That childhood shyness returned. No longer did I have the safety of working out in my garage. Knowing Drew would be at the gym provided the same calmness that walking to high school with my friend did years ago.

By the time I was comfortable at the gym, Drew announced he was leaving the gym to start his own workout facility. Naturally, I was thrilled for Drew, but I was sad for myself. On his last night at the gym, I brought in a cake. As members would come into the gym, they'd stop to take a piece or at least say goodbye to Drew.

Early evening inside xCellFitness.

ME

I'm sorry you are leaving. In the beginning I was terrified to come into this place, but I knew everything would be okay when I saw you here.

DREW

I've seen great strides in changing attitudes since you've been coming here. You deserve the credit for that.

ME

Thank you.

DREW

I never asked you, how was the dinner with Megan and Lee?

ME

Horrible. They stuck to themselves. Eventually, at ten o'clock, they left. They couldn't be having any fun; I know I wasn't.

DREW

I should have warned you they don't know how to socialize outside their gym element. I am sorry I couldn't make it.

ME

It's not your fault. I cooked up a storm and invited my wonderful friends from the area. I don't think Lee or Megan appreciated any of the effort, expense, or other guests. I get the feeling they are used to people doing and buying things for them because they are good looking. At least everyone else had fun.

DREW

You're a nice guy, Tom. Be careful of them.

ME

(puzzled)

You are the third person to recently warn me about them. One person told me their interest in me was as deep as my pockets. When I remarked to someone else that I thought Megan and Lee were good people, I was told, "They aren't what you think they are."

DREW

This is a very incestuous group. I've been here a long time and have seen too much.

ME

I guess it's time to start working out. I just love muscle burn. Feels similar to the burn I get when I urinate!

DREW

(not getting the joke)

Thank you for the cake. Don't forget every Sunday we have an open house spaghetti dinner. You are welcome anytime.

As Drew and I shake hands, Megan walks past us with two of her trainees.

MEGAN

(talking to her trainees)

Can you believe that Lee had taken that bitch home and *fucked her on my bed*? I told Earl if he fired her, I would work her weekend hours until he found a replacement.

ME

(after they passed, to Drew)

Oh my God, he's cured. Parents everywhere now have hope for their gay sons! Get him on Oprah!

When Drew left xCellFitness, part of the gym's moral fiber collapsed. It just isn't the same. Nobody with his combination of warmth, integrity, or charisma fills his void. Eventually I learned that some shoes can't be filled, so it's not worth wasting the time to look.

23 Keep the Faith: Brian's Update

It's dark outside Equilibrium, and Barbara and I are sitting on the low-rise brick wall separating the parking lot from the sidewalk. I love to sit on that wall and often retreat there when the dance music is too loud or the bar is too crowded. That area is also a frequent hangout for smokers from both the bar and the adjoining small businesses in the complex, a perfect spot for Barbara to keep an eye on the parking lot and yet remain close enough to quickly enter the bar if needed.

BARBARA

Barbara lights a cigarette.
Don't tell anyone.

ME

Won't need to. Everyone can see.

BARBARA

Patty is bending the bar seats. Have you noticed how
two or three of them lean inward?

ME

No, but you'd better get them reinforced with steel.
Speaking of Patty, what happened last night?

BARBARA

I didn't realize Patty showed up drunk to judge the drag
show. She continued drinking during the show until
about three quarters through when she put her head
down on a table and passed out. Four contestants cursed
me and walked out.

ME

That's awful. It could have been much worse. When she was passed out and the spotlight shined on her, could you see her roots?

BARBARA

(laughing)
No!

ME

Good thing. Some mean fag would have taken a picture.

BARBARA

Only you!

ME

(laughing)
How long was she passed out?

BARBARA

By last call her husband was able to get her to the car. I should have known something was wrong. She was too quiet when she came in. Never again.

ME

Look, everyone knows how she is. The surprise isn't that she was drunk, but that her hair was done. How's Brian doing in the PT class?

BARBARA

He said the course was tough. He has to memorize all the muscle groups and doesn't think he can do it.

ME

He'll be just fine, you just watch. I've heard him rattle off decades of sports statistics. Some statistics date back to before they were wearing helmets and cups.

Since many of my local friends smoked, sitting on the wall was a convenient location for socializing opportunities throughout the night. I was not surprised when Brian not only memorized all the muscle groups, he passed the PT course with ease. We all were delighted, especially Barbara.

24 D-I-V-O-R-C-E

Judy and I were on adjacent treadmills with me just starting while Judy was cooling down. By now word had gotten out about Lee and Megan's divorce. Surprisingly, they both continued to use xCellFitness. Interestingly, everyone had a genuine concern about how Lee was holding up, perhaps because he was generally unreadable and very unapproachable. But not once did I hear anyone express concern about how Megan was faring during these no doubt difficult times.

On treadmills.

JUDY

Everyone is worried about Lee now that he is going through his divorce. Lee had a cow when word got back to him that Roland was asking how he was doing. He let Roland have it.

ME

Yeah, I didn't fare any better. I asked Keith how Lee was doing, and within a day or two, Lee came over to me and said, "If you have a question about me, you ask me. Got it?" Sad that so many good people are concerned about Lee, and he just ignores them. He treats his car better than his friends.

JUDY

I am more concerned about Victoria. Have you noticed her lately? She looks like a skeleton again and continues to say she is too fat. She told me she ran into some guy from high school who told her she looked great, but she didn't believe him. You'd think that would have awakened her. She is beyond hope.

ME

We need to keep trying.

25 A Natural What?

One evening I was sitting at the gym's round table post-workout, reading the paper. In a rare move, Lee came up from behind me and started talking to me.

> LEE
> Why do you associate with Brian? He's bad news.
> ME
> I know his grandmother. She's a good person, so I know he's got good in him somewhere. (thinking about Lee and Megan, I added:) Besides, if I stayed away from everyone I was warned about, I wouldn't associate with anyone.

From my interactions with Brian and my exposure to Lee, I thought they'd be great friends if they got to know each other and saw what I see in both of them. But after Lee made his comment, I figured I wouldn't suggest, encourage, or set up such an opportunity for a fulfilling friendship to occur.

> LEE
> Have you ever considered doing a bodybuilding show? *You'd be a natural.* I could train you.

I was shocked at the question, since I never expressed any interest in doing a show, nor do I have any real athletic ability. Surprisingly I didn't laugh at the suggestion. So I concluded he was only after the training money.

ME
No. I would be so embarrassed wearing posing briefs.
Nobody wants to see my milk duds. It should be
obvious that I am not athletic.

The thoughts of a bodybuilding show triggered old insecurities about my athletic deficiencies and memories of high school physical education class. Basketball wasn't the only sport I suffered through. It was all of them, really. And, of course, physical education class, five days a week in high school, only accentuated the deficiency instead of decreasing it.

For most sports in physical education class, the students chose their own teams. We'd sit in lines on the gym floor until we were picked. Once picked, we would stand behind the team captain who selected us. Naturally, the team captains picked the jocks first, followed by the athletic guys. Usually, I had a long wait; I was always one of the last five picked but, thankfully, never the last one. Although at that point it didn't matter; the team selection process was a character-building experience that greatly contributed toward mine.

In a way, you have to laugh about the way physical education classes were structured. With such varied sporting skill sets and aptitudes among the students, it wasn't like everyone could become skilled in the three or so weeks allocated for a particular sport. For any given sport I had the same performance at the beginning of the three-week period as I did at the end. In fact, for *every* sport I had *exactly* the same performance during my entire four years of high school. And rest assured it wasn't exemplary.

At the end of the three-week time frame for each sport, we had to take a physical test. You can imagine how well I did. My goal was never to do well in the test, as that was never going to happen. Instead, my goal was not to embarrass myself with form or function during the test.

By far the most memorable test was the football test in my senior year. The football test consisted of measuring how far you could throw the football. Although it sounds reasonable, at that age my fingers couldn't even grip the fully inflated football. For me it was like trying to palm a watermelon.

As the guy ahead of me grabbed a football, everyone moved deep into the field. He threw the ball longer than I could kick it, assuming I actually made foot contact.

Expectedly, when it was my turn, everyone moved in close. Real close. Close enough to pass a joint if they had one. Then, as I started the motion to throw the ball—praying I would not drop it—from the infield a friend, who was just like me, including his lack of athletic abilities, yelled:

"Tom, give it all your effort!"

I almost died. I laughed so hard my throw landed even shorter than I had anticipated—it landed several feet in front of the closest infielder. Thankfully, the ball didn't bounce backward toward me.

I remember one more thing about that friend who yelled to me during the football throw. I saw him at a high school reunion. It was a blast. We were transported back in time, and the comments flew. One of the reunion highlights occurred when a male classmate won a bottle of wine for having the most kids. I stated rather loudly, "Wine? With six kids, give him a box of condoms!" My friend turned to me and said, "You haven't changed a bit." Actually, I have, but not in the ways that are important. Can't wait for the next reunion.

In all fairness, the two major reasons for my lack of athletic prowess were my shyness and the influence of my step-grandfather. He would repeatedly say, "Bodily exercise profits little," which, looking back, is interesting because he loved watching sports and even played some! Maybe he lost money betting on the games. Since he was also the person who got me listening to Loretta Lynn, which opened the door to country music for me, I can't be too upset with him.

Recalling these experiences as I considered entering a bodybuilding competition, I felt the return of the old gym class anxiety I experienced growing up. In addition, I also feared how I'd look in posing briefs—I most certainly wouldn't look like the gray sweatpants guy! Of course, at my age, this bodybuilding show certainly wasn't going to make me or break me. But nobody wants to be embarrassed or potentially ridiculed at any stage of life.

26 Way of the World

Cynthia is always getting on me about being too generous. The way I see it is I have been lucky in life. Yes, I work hard and live frugally. But I also realize that, as tough as I may have it, other people may not be as fortunate or lucky. In one way or another, people have down periods. Perhaps if I show compassion to others, they will return the compassion to someone else. That's the way of the world. And if they don't? Well, that's a reflection on them, not me. I think my country music heroes would agree.

I am in xCellFitness performing bicep curls on the cable machine. On an adjacent machine, a friendly member was performing seated back extensions. During our simultaneously occurring minute break, we start talking.

GYM MEMBER 2

I am really bummed. My cat is at the vet and needs a twelve-hundred-dollar operation. The operation is not guaranteed to be successful.

ME

That's too bad. I'm sorry to hear it.

GYM MEMBER 2

I need to sell my stuff to help raise money for the operation. If the cat dies from not having an operation, I'll never forgive myself.

I continue to work out on the cable machine by performing various sets of bicep and tricep exercises. Finally, I go on my knees for ab exercises. Not completely finished with my ab workout, I leave the gym and return about ten minutes later. I go over to the cat owner.

ME

I went to two ATMs, and the most I could get is six hundred dollars toward your cat's operation.

GYM MEMBER 2

Oh, thank you. But I can't pay you back.

ME

That's okay, it's a gift. I had pets growing up, and I know what they meant to me. Your kids will be devastated if your cat dies.

GYM MEMBER 2

Thank you.

27 PEE

Cynthia and I are carrying our purchased lunches down the long corridor from the cafeteria.

CYNTHIA

We need to sit in your area. They filled the vacant desk next to me this morning.

ME

No problem. Too bad they walked that contractor out. I liked her.

CYNTHIA

Yeah, she should have never asked our manager if he had ever done this sort of work before. I guess she got tired of the circles he sent her on.

ME

She was too experienced for this place. I miss sitting together, but I'm glad neither one of us has to listen to Elaine and her bag of games anymore.

CYNTHIA

Get this. My new neighbor introduced himself. He told me he was a member of the Mensa club.

ME

How long did it take him to figure out the speed limit is higher than the average IQ around here?

CYNTHIA

And that's in a school zone with yellow lights flashing!

ME

I've been studying the steroid guys since the New Year's party. It's like they are stuck, mentally, in the time period when they started bodybuilding. As if whatever situation they were facing wasn't or hasn't fully been dealt with, just sidetracked. Mentally, they still have the same fears, fears that are now hidden by their muscular frames.

Finally, we get to my work area, and I point to a vacant seat directly across the aisle.

ME

Cynthia, sit over there. That cube is vacant.

These work areas are very old and much larger than the cubes we previously sat in. They are arranged in a pair of *U*'s [UU] with a desk in the curved part and a shared table on the adjacent arm between two consecutive *U*'s. We sit across the aisle from each other and turn the chairs to face the aisle and each other. We put our food on the shared tables.

Cynthia and I sit and start opening the food containers. I turn to unlock my computer and start typing.

CYNTHIA

If you're going to start working, I'm going back to my desk.

ME

No, I'm not working. I'm looking to see if it's Lee's birthday today.

Cynthia rolls her eyes as she eats.

ME

(speaking as I type)

Last August I was sitting at the gym table. Lee came up to me and in a childish voice—like nobody loved him— said, "Today is my birthday." So I was sitting there thinking that something is very wrong here. Everyone is worried about him, and he's acting like nobody cares … which wasn't the case. So I figured I'd do something about it the next year. The time has come.

CYNTHIA

So he talked to you when you were captive and he was not? He must want something.

ME

(still typing and looking at the monitor)
Naturally, I have forgotten which day in the month is the actual birthday. So I go on a people-finder website every day to see when his age changes.

Cynthia rolls her eyes again while eating.

ME

It only takes a second. Um, not today.

With that daily ritual concluded, I turn to my food.

ME

I wanted to give him a surprise party to show him that he has friends who care about him regardless of his issues and struggles. But the problem I couldn't solve was, "How will he understand that these people are offering the unique gift of a lifetime of love … and not just birthday greetings?" So instead, at the beginning of the month, I gave Keith three hundred dollars to do something special for Lee … under the condition that Lee not know it came from me.

CYNTHIA

(swallowing her food and whispering from across the aisle)
Are you shitting me?

ME

So when I first began socializing with Lee and Megan, I was afraid that Lee would beat me up for sending flowers to his wife.

CYNTHIA

Wait a minute. Why would you send flowers to another man's wife?

ME

I send Loretta Lynn roses.

Cynthia looks incredulous.

ME

I had gone home for lunch one day and there was a phone message from the guy I was dating. He said he was breaking up with me. No explanation or reason. Nothing, just goodbye. He couldn't even tell me in person. I was upset about it all day long. So that night in the gym …

I was on the elliptical machine. Right in front of me on the recumbent bike, Lee was having a good ol' time laughing and chatting away with a young lady sitting next to him. In the mirrors I spotted Megan coming from behind us, and I could see she was mad as hell. I knew it wasn't going to be good. Megan went by me and stopped in front of Lee with downward extended arms as if to say, "What about me?" Then she huffed off. Later I looked over, and she was sitting at the table crying. I can't tell you how bad I felt for her. It totally eclipsed my breakup misery.

So that night I went to bed, and I couldn't sleep. Finally, after hours of just lying there, I realized I couldn't sleep because I was shocked at the sight of seeing a strong woman cry. In the middle of the night, I got up, went to my computer, and ordered her flowers.

CYNTHIA

She must have loved the flowers. What did she say when she thanked you?

ME

I didn't give my name. I was afraid Lee would beat me
up. All I wrote on the card was, "Your smile brightens
up our gym," which seemed kind of stupid because I
can't ever recall her smiling or laughing at the gym.

CYNTHIA

Yes, that was stupid. I wouldn't have gotten involved,
but you don't listen to me. One day someone will take
your good intentions the wrong way. You'd better learn
a self-defense tactic. Try PEE.

ME

As in pee my pants?

I start to eat my lunch as Cynthia pushes her finished meal aside. We
are still seated facing each other across the aisle.

CYNTHIA

PEE. The P stands for package. As in kick 'em in the
package.

Cynthia has been sitting with her legs crossed. She kicks her top leg in
my direction.

Then, as they go down, you grab 'em by the esophagus.
Cynthia demonstrates by taking her arm in a *V* and putting it
around the front of her neck. Her legs are still crossed. I am laughing
hysterically.

CYNTHIA

Finally—poke 'em in the eyes!

Cynthia displays the poking motion by thrusting her right arm
forward and backward several times with bent index and middle
fingers while the other three fingers are tucked under her palm. I am
laughing so hard I am practically choking on my food.

CYNTHIA

Remember it's P-E-E. Package, esophagus, eyes. And
don't you forget it.

And I haven't and neither should you!

28 Tuna and Butterflies

There is an unwritten rule in the gym: never warm up smelly food. It is basic gym etiquette similar to wiping down cardio equipment after usage. I walk into the gym and immediately notice an overpowering stench. No doubt the agonizing expression on my face shows my displeasure at this condition. I scan my gym identification.

Troy is at the front counter, complaining about the smell.

TROY

Can you please have someone open both the front and rear doors? The tuna stench is overpowering.

FRONT COUNTER WORKER

I can't leave the front counter. I'll ask Anthony to do it when he returns.

Troy and I start walking toward the equipment together.

ME

This is ridiculous.

TROY

Yep. It was like this last night too.

ME

Now you know why I don't date women!

TROY

Tom, those are the women you stay away from.

ME

That Facebook posting your girlfriend wrote was very

nice. I wanted to comment, but I wasn't sure how my comment would be taken.

TROY

Which post? She's always posting shit.

ME

That after ten years of being together, she still gets butterflies whenever she's around you.

TROY

Yeah.

ME

I was going to write "Me too."

TROY

(laughing)

You should have, I would have laughed.

I pause at the round table as Troy keeps walking to resume his workout.

Dennis, a wise and well-respected gym member and a former US Special Forces officer, is already seated. He is a hulking man with a quiet and steady demeanor. People often ask Dennis his opinion and in return get a well-thought-out and insightful response. Nobody messes with Dennis.

It's always a pleasure to see Dennis, and I greet him as I sit to prepare for my workout. In the back corner of the gym I spot the lady whose cat needed an operation. Even from a distance her new boob job is evident. Although I am surprised to see it, she does look great with them. It was money well spent.

Megan is nearby, training a group of young females; they are doing leg exercises requiring a lot of jumping and knee bends. Curious gym members watch with amusement and bewilderment. Dennis has been intently watching their workout, which is now almost finished.

ME

Dennis, are you watching the show?

DENNIS

I have no clue what she is having them do or the value it provides.

ME

Kind of looks like a frog jump.

DENNIS

These young women will have ruined knees by their thirties if this keeps up.

ME

Great way to reduce my competition.

With the training over, one of Megan's trainees comes over to get her gym bag next to the table. She sits down in the vacant seat next to Dennis and wipes herself off with a towel from her bag.

MEGAN'S TRAINEE

Dennis, what do you think about my training?

DENNIS

Young lady, I'm not going to say anything with your trainer just over there. Listen to your body and trust your own intuition.

MEGAN'S TRAINEE

Thank you.

She leaves.

ME

Dennis, why didn't you tell her?

DENNIS

Just the fact she was asking meant she was questioning it. She'll come to the right conclusion. No need for me to comment. But I will comment that three more people left the gym because of her trainer.

ME

Why?

DENNIS

Complaints Earl refuses to do anything about. Megan's
training sessions are interfering with member workouts.
Who wants to go to a gym not knowing if there will be
any available equipment?

ME

There is plenty of equipment here for everybody. Megan
interferes with workouts intentionally.

Leaving the table, I walk over to the elliptical machines, noticing the
member arrival of Megan's next class. Several women from the just-
completed session are chatting with Megan in front of the posing
room.

On the elliptical machines, Victoria is between me and Judy. Victoria
turns to me.

VICTORIA

They're staring at me.

ME

Who?

VICTORIA

Megan's girls.

ME

And they should. You look great. They are paying her all
that money, and you were smart enough to go back to
training yourself.

Victoria and I continue our conversation, which becomes more
disturbing by the minute. Judy overhears our conversation, and from
behind Victoria, mouths her thoughts.

JUDY

(moving her lips only)

She's gone. Gone.

After a couple of minutes of conversation, I realize Victoria is getting
worse and not better. I notice Jay working out on the cable machines.
Jay has a teenage daughter, so I figure he could potentially give

me advice on someone having body image issues. I end my cardio abruptly and head over to where Jay is performing bicep exercises. He listens to me, but does not acknowledge, look at, or speak to me before finishing his set.

ME

Jay, Victoria's in trouble. She said her first priority was not gaining any weight. She's got two little kids. She needs to get her priorities right. She won't listen to me.

Jay finishes after a few reps.

JAY

Here is what we'll do. I'll ask her for naked pictures. That'll build up her self-esteem.

ME

(acting surprised and unsure of the tactic)
Okay. If you think that's best. Thank you.

Jay resumes working out, and I start my workout at the other end of the gym.

I didn't like Jay's strategy but sometimes you've got to go with the flow and hope for the best. So that's exactly what I did.

29 Colliding Worlds

Equilibrium is the only connection I have to the local gay community. I value my time there. It is my sanctuary from the injustices and inequalities of a world I fight five days a week. Despite advocating diversity, surprisingly, I was not thrilled when Brian brought select "A-list" gym members into the bar. Specifically, I didn't like exposing this part of my life to a group I suspected didn't understand or appreciate it. Let me make it clear, I had no delusions that any of them would convert to my team! But I have to admit, watching them react to my environment was fascinating and memorable.

Inside Equilibrium, early evening just after several "A-list" gym members, including Megan, arrive. Brian is celebrating his new career as a personal trainer in our gym. I am delighted for Brian but wish they would celebrate somewhere else.

BRIAN

Man, can't believe next month I'm meeting up with the old party group. The great times we had.

ME

That can't be good.

TIM

This is some place your family has here. Can I look around?

BRIAN

Sure. It gets packed around ten or eleven.

Tim wanders off.

BRIAN

What does everyone want to drink? It's on me to
celebrate becoming a certified personal trainer and my
new job.

Brian texts the drink orders to the bartender.

ME

What a great business concept, owning a gay bar.
Instead of throwing expensive backyard barbecues,
invite your friends to a bar and make money off them.

KEITH

(turning his head looking around the room)
Lee would never come into a place like this.

Megan nods her head affirmatively.

BRIAN

Tom's in love with Lee.

MEGAN

What?

I am so embarrassed. What would make him say that? I exhibit a
pained look on my face.

Fortunately, no one pays attention to Brian's comment.

BRIAN

Here comes Terri. Let me introduce you.

Terri, Brian's girlfriend, enters and joins the group.

TERRI

Terri hugs Brian and me.

Hi.

Tim returns from his walk around the establishment.

BRIAN

Terri, this is Tim, Keith, and Megan from the gym.

TIM

(with astonishment)
That guy over there just hit on me!

Brian, Terri, and I look at each other and smile. We realize Tim was referring to Matt, the woman with the glued-on mustache dressed in guy's clothing, who had fooled Tim.

ME

Who wouldn't? I know I exhibit remarkable self-restraint whenever I am around you.

BRIAN

(laughing)

What do you want to drink, Tim?

TIM

Gin and tonic—double.

Brian goes off to get the drinks.

TERRI

(to Megan)

I've heard so much about you. You look great for your age.

Megan gives her an icy stare.

ME

She looks great for any age!

Annoyed, Megan leaves us and walks over to the other gym members, Keith and Tim.

Brian returns with the drinks. Once he distributes the drinks, he joins the gym group, leaving me alone to talk to Terri.

It appears that Brian may have had some sort of hair restoration work performed at some point, and many people have questioned it. Terri thought she'd get the scoop from me since it's seldom just the two of us.

TERRI

(to me)

Does Brian have plugs?

ME

I am in the "gay mindset" and taking the diplomatic approach.

I don't know what's on his shopping list.

TERRI

Terri stares at me as if the question should be obvious and not
understanding my answer.

Plugs?

ME

(as if a revelation is made)

Oh, you mean hair plugs.

TERRI

What did you think I meant?

ME

(smartly)

Butt plugs.

Terri bursts out with laughter and walks outside so as not to draw
more attention to herself indoors. Through the windows I see she is
still laughing outdoors.

Fortunately, once the free drinks were finished the gym members left. Life
resumed in my sanctuary. They never again appeared at the bar while I was
there.

30 Naked Pictures

I spotted Victoria in the gym for the first time since I talked to Jay about her. I had no idea if Jay had followed through or, as I had hoped, changed his approach regarding asking Victoria for naked pictures. At the end of my workout, I walked over to the vacant treadmill next to Victoria. As I was programming the machine, I started talking to her.

ME

Anything new with you?

VICTORIA

(excitedly)

You're not going to believe this. Jay asked me for naked pictures.

ME

(acting surprised)

Really? (sounding incredulous) Sorry, I didn't mean it like that. That's impressive; he could have any woman. Are you going to do it?

VICTORIA

(quickly and dismissively)

Nah. I'm a mother. I can't be doing stuff like that.

ME

Here's what you do, Victoria. Ask Jay for naked pictures of himself. Then forward them to me.

Cheryl, another gym member with whom I had become friendly, comes over and gets on the treadmill on the other side of me. She is angry. I turn and nod to her while talking to Victoria. Victoria spots one of the hot muscle guys, Rod, working out. Rod had been dating Megan since her divorce from Lee.

VICTORIA

Not that Jay isn't handsome, but I'd really like to hang with Rod.

ME

So ask him out. You've got the goods. You look great. Go for it.

VICTORIA

He'd never go out with someone like me. I can't compete with Megan.

ME

Wake up, Victoria. It's easy. Just smile and put your best girl forward.

ME

(to Cheryl)
That was a fast workout.

CHERYL

I couldn't use the machines. Wherever I went that bitch sent her girls to work in with me. I can't wait five minutes between sets. There are other machines she could have had them use. After the second machine with that nonsense, I just gave up.

31 You Gotta Do What You Gotta Do

One night, I was sitting alone at the gym's round table looking at the newspaper. Not long after I sat down, Lee's bodybuilder friends, who had just finished their workout, joined me.

ME

You're here late tonight.

KEITH

(puts his gym bag on the table and sits down)

Big game tomorrow, so we doubled up tonight.

(pulls his wallet and car keys out of the gym bag)

Presently, Troy, Ted, Peter, and Jay come over with protein shakes.

KEITH

(stands and grabs his things)

Guys, I've got to get home.

The guys say various departure comments to Keith. They sit in the three empty seats with one guy left standing.

ME

Where's Lee? It's surprising he's not here with you.

TED

He had to run some errand with Megan. I don't get it. They are divorced. Megan needs to find some other patsy. Remember when she used to come in here and yell at him in front of everyone? He probably wished he were dead, yet he never said a thing. Amazing how she zaps the confidence and happiness out of everyone.

TROY

I would have moved far away from her after divorcing.

TED

Ted leans inward to the table and speaks in a soft and sincere voice.
I think Lee is "challenged."

TROY

No, I wouldn't say "challenged." I'd say "limited."

PETER

It's Megan's fault. She is so fucking selfish and self-centered. She always has to be the center of attention. She is so in love with herself.

TED

Yep. Can you imagine being married to her? It's bad enough seeing her in here. Can you imagine what she's like the other twenty-two hours a day?

TROY

(nods his head in agreement)

TED

Nah, it's deeper than Megan. Something from childhood.

PETER

Have you ever noticed Lee only talks about sports, cars, and comic strips? Everything else is off-limits.

ME

That's sad.

JAY

Look, Tom. We've all known Lee a long time. Nobody cares whether he's gay, straight, bisexual, or asexual. We just want him happy. He very well could be gay or just gay to get away. If it came down to a life of matrimonial hell or being gay for a couple of months to gain my freedom, I'd be the biggest fag on the planet. You gotta do what you gotta do.

ME

Stick with what you know. I don't need your
competition, it's tough enough already. Have you ever
tried to help Lee?

Everyone laughs but me. Sadly, they were not laughing at my
competition remark but at my helping remark.

ME

Well, why not? We all live here together and will grow
old together; therefore, we should all help each other
out.

And, as a man who practices what he preaches, that was the start of Project
Lee or, abbreviated, P-Lee. It was a simple idea: make Lee realize that he
is loved. His life would be so much more enriched through the love of his
friends and knowing that people care about him and are always there to
help him carry his burdens. Maybe then he'd be able to smile and laugh
through the storms of life. If his friends weren't able to help or didn't know
how to help, then fine, I would.

There was one item I had to immediately address: I had to ignore any
remark about Lee being gay. The fact was, unless he had the confidence to
ask me out and be public about any relationship, his sexual orientation was
irrelevant to me. With that decided, my sleep immediately improved.

That simple yet abstract plan turned into a complete nightmare to execute. Too bad Lee's project couldn't be solved using dog treats or by taking
personal trainer courses.

32 Jack Discovers Love

After months of feeding Jack dog biscuits, I knew I was making great progress on several fronts. He'd stopped barking at me as I came and went. When he saw me in my yard, he'd start barking to let me know he was outside. And, more impressively, he'd bark ferociously when strangers were in my yard. Even though he seemed to accept me as a friend, I still stood back from the fence for safety.

Sheila's backyard fence just before dusk.

ME

Here you go, Jack.

Jack takes the treat in his mouth, leaves the fence, and walks several feet away. Surprisingly, Jack drops the treat without eating it and returns to the fence where I am standing. He puts his front paws on the top of the fence. At that moment I realized Jack wanted to be petted; being loved was more important than eating.

ME

(while cautiously petting Jack)

Ah, good puppy. You want some lovin'.

That was the day Jack discovered love, at least with me, and Project Jack was closed. I was never afraid of Jack again.

33 They're Here!

The most admirable quality about the gay bar is how friendly and tolerant everyone is toward one other. I used to look around and think, "This is the way every place should be."

With diversity comes a type of patron that I personally don't care for—those that are there to "use" the guys. It's one thing for straights to visit a gay bar because it's generally a happening place, friendly and safe. But it's an entirely different situation when straights repeatedly visit the gay bar and intentionally upset long-established relationships for their own selfish benefit. I call these individuals *fag nags*. And it's even worse when these fag nags try to "lead" us. Don't they realize we are descendants of Alexander the Great? I must be clear that I exclude *fag hags* from the fag nag group. If you don't know the definition of a fag hag or understand the fag hag/gay guy relationship, the best example is Jack and Karen on the TV show *Will & Grace*; otherwise you can look the up definition on the internet. One important distinction is a fag hag is of female gender whereas a fag nag can be either male or female.

It was a typical Saturday night, and I had decided to sit at a table rather than the bar. I had reoriented the chair to face the bar. This seating position exposed the fact that my legs were crossed. I was reading the gay newspaper I'd pick up at the front door. I could hear Lyle talking to the customers seated at the bar.

Equilibrium's phone rings.

Lyle answers it.

LYLE

Equilibrium. (pause) No, they aren't here.

Lyle hangs up the phone and speaks to the customers.

Look at the way Tom is sitting. He must have a small
dick.

ME

I overhear the remark and move to a vacant bar seat while retorting:

Looking at you, Lyle, is more effective than cold water
immersion.

A few customers laugh.

LYLE

That's not nice.

ME

You started it.

In walk the infamous Arnold and Randall. Finally, "they're here."
Regardless of the season, Arnold always wears a black, three-piece
suit and coordinated tie as though he just attended a funeral or just
finished door-to-door religious solicitations. Arnold's shiny shaved
scalp and distinguished white-haired goatee do little to mask his deep
facial crevices. Sadly, Arnold's youthful years spent in the sun without
protection or moisturizer resulted in a face with more deep cracks
than my sidewalk.

Similarly, Randall is consistently dressed in a pair of stretched
chinos and a horizontally striped Izod shirt. Depending on the
coloring, sometimes Randall's shirt gives his upper body a globe
like resemblance. Randall prominently displays several hanging
chains from his neck and proudly brags they were inherited family
heirlooms. Disbelieving, the guys joke behind his back that he
probably bought tin chains by the inch and spray painted them
gold. Of course, my assessment tends to be more memorable and
potentially accurate when I ask, "I wonder which anal beads Randall
will be wearing tonight?" Yes, I realize statements like that lower my
W-Factor into the negative numbers, but the humor helps alleviate
the difficulties encountered when they are around. Randall constantly

boasts about his perfect vision as he approaches his senior citizen years, yet he is blind to his awful hairstyle Lyle once described as a "decayed roadkill-looking toupee."

While Arnold and Randall may consider themselves two prominent Pawtucket homosexuals, many consider them assholes for their arrogance, combative style (with others and each other), and superior attitudes. Stories of their behavior spread quickly in the Pawtucket community, with the local food and beverage services staff members labeling them as *two flakes in a drift*. They have been together a long time and, thankfully, they are removed from the dating pool. Randall can be very nice prior to drinking, but he doesn't handle alcohol well.

When Lyle, the bartender, spots Arnold and Randall entering the bar, he pours six shots and places them along the back counter. When Arnold and Randall aren't looking, Lyle will discreetly drink a shot or two before each interaction with them.

Randall has already had a drink or two prior to entering the bar, and although he is not drunk, his vocal delivery and shuffling walk reflect a near-intoxicated condition.

LYLE
(drinks a shot with his back turned)
Already working on it.
Arnold hugs and kisses me.

ARNOLD
What cologne are you wearing? It smells vaguely familiar.

ME
(pauses)
Anal Ease with a splash of PAM.
No one laughs, not even a smile! I thought that was a great comment. I guess even Joan Rivers had lines that bombed too.

ARNOLD
Nice. This is an upscale establishment.

                          ME
This is a gay bar with condoms and lube by the front
door.
(looking at my half-filled appletini)
Lyle, I'm going to need another one.
                        RANDALL
(loudly)
Arnold, if Jeremy comes in, I'm going to ask that he
discuss payment arrangements with us. He isn't a slow
pay, he's a no pay.
                        ARNOLD
Randall, I agree we need to discuss a payment plan with
him, but this isn't the appropriate time or place to talk
about it.
                        RANDALL
All I'm saying is we aren't a charity. I've already talked to
him a few weeks ago, and he hasn't made a payment.
Luckily for us, Randall notices an unfamiliar face next to him and
introduces himself, ending the argument.
                        RANDALL
(to unfamiliar individual)
So are you new in town? Here is our card. We are the
premier designers and antique dealers in the area. We
cater to everyone. Please keep our card handy and refer
us to your friends. People can afford more than they
think. We have offices in Pawtucket, Providence, and
Central Falls. We can help determine a budget and
will have your place looking fit for the Rockefellers,
Huxtables, or even the Flintstones...
Everyone has heard Randall and Arnold's spiel many times. Referring
to the new person, the guy on my left whispers "Are you going to save
him?" to which I shake my head negatively.

During Randall's solicitation, I hear Patty, the female half of a straight, middle-aged couple, at the far end of the bar. The heavyset wife is very opinionated to the point of displaying a great lapse in social decorum—she talks as if she means to throw darts at other people before they can throw them at her (which they never do). She enjoys being the center of attention. Her laughing and excessively loud voice can be heard all throughout the bar which annoys other customers. Her retired military ex-fighter pilot husband looks like a professional boxer and thus provides additional, unofficial bar security should it be needed.

I suspect Patty's husband gets dragged to the bar to please his wife, so I feel sorry for him. Once I asked him if, as a teenager, he thought he'd grow up to spend his nights at a gay bar. Patty's husband, of course, said, "No." I responded, "Neither did I."

PATTY

(loudly)

Oh my God. The bride had a ferret face. You'd think she'd try to embellish the few, okay, the one good feature she had. Instead, she stood at the altar looking like she had just come up from the burrow.

(laughing)

And the dress? Did nothing for her flat chest. If I'd have been her, I would have stuffed myself with water balloons.

(pointing to her large breasts and laughing loudly)

Fortunately, I don't need them with these melons.

While Patty talks the guy to my left holds his drink by his mouth and repeats the phrase "Shut up" several times. Not that she could possibly hear him or that hearing him would stop her. I am getting annoyed at yet another of Patty's loud, unflattering descriptions and opinions as though Patty, or any of us, has any right to judge. I am certain the bride did her best on one of the happiest days of her life.

ME

(to Lyle)

I hate it when they come in. This is our environment, our sanctuary, a place where we hide from the injustices and expectations of the world and just be ourselves. Not show time for the lonely straights.

LYLE

I like it when they come in. They tip 100 percent.

I look back down the bar at Patty. She is leaning down as she talks to her neighbors, and her large breasts, although partially hidden within her loose blouse, are resting on the bar and seemingly pointed in opposite directions.

ME

(matter-of-factly)

Well, she should spend some of that tip money on better-supporting undergarments. One girl is facing the Atlantic Ocean; the other is pointing toward the Pacific!

ARNOLD

(sitting on my right, spoken very condescendingly as though reprimanding)

Look, Patty would be hurt if she heard you say that. She has gained a lot of weight lately, and I'm sure it's a touchy subject.

ME

Just one minute. It has nothing to do with her weight. It's about undergarment support. She shouldn't brag about something she doesn't support.

Arnold gives me a look.

ME

Don't look at me that way. If she can't take it, she shouldn't dish it out.

I look back at Patty. She is sitting upright but sagging.

ME

Don't her ta-tas remind you of Slinkys?

ARNOLD

(scolding)

You are so incorrigible.

The phone rings, and Lyle answers.

LYLE

Equilibrium.

(long pause)

Yes, they are here.

(laughing)

Did you want to talk to them?

The caller hangs up. Lyle smiles as he returns the phone to it's charging base.

34 P-Lee

It took me three weeks to formulate the Project Lee plan. One of the tougher problems to solve was figuring out how to be around Lee long enough to execute any sort of plan since he seemed so uncomfortable around me. It weighed heavily on my mind until I recalled Lee mentioning he could train me for a bodybuilding show. After all, in Lee's own words, I was "a natural." Although I had no real interest in doing a show, paying Lee to train me seemed like a win-win proposition for us: Lee would make money, and I would teach him about love while I move a step closer toward looking like the "after" photo. So, for better or most likely worse, I was going to do a bodybuilding show. Yippee.

At the end of the day, I appear at Cynthia's desk unannounced.
Cynthia is on the phone and signals me to wait a minute.

> CYNTHIA
> Okay, I'll make the changes tomorrow morning and
> email them to you. You'll have it by nine o'clock in the
> morning. You're welcome.

Cynthia hangs up the phone.

> What brings you to my area?

> ME
> I've decided to do an all-natural bodybuilding contest. I
> was just over at Ryan's desk going over my supplement
> list.

Ryan is a coworker from one of our previous work areas. A recent college graduate, Ryan is hoping one day to turn his fitness avocation into a profession by opening his own gym. He certainly understands everything there is to know about training for a bodybuilding show.

CYNTHIA

All natural as in nude?

ME

No, all natural as in Breyer's. No steroids and stuff like that.

CYNTHIA

Are you crazy? Why all of a sudden would you want to do that?

ME

Well, I figure it can't be too bad. I've already dieted a couple of times and trained with personal trainers. The only thing that's new is posing. How bad can it be?

CYNTHIA

(realizing the truth)

Is your trainer Lee?

ME

Yes.

Cynthia shakes her head sideways and starts to pack up her desk as she talks.

CYNTHIA

I don't think you've thought this through. Look, these people are bottom-feeders, just stringing you along trying to profit from your good nature.

ME

Maybe so. Whether Lee is gay or not is none of my business. He needs to understand that he is a rich man. He's got friends who love him, care about him, and want to see him happy. He largely ignores or misinterprets their concern. I know these people; they are good people. He should be proud they are his friends. Perhaps with their love he can overcome whatever demons he is fighting. I will make it obvious

to him. As for me, I've been wanting to take my
bodybuilding further. So it's mutually beneficial.

CYNTHIA

Then he should be paying you. I wouldn't waste one
cent or one minute on Lee or Megan. But I've noticed
when it comes to other people, you have an open wallet.
Let's add it up:

You spent what, a thousand dollars on dinners and
training so Brian could become a personal trainer?
Then there's that time you gave that lady six hundred
dollars as a "gift" to help cure her "sick" cat. Funny, she
probably spent it on her boobs instead. And what about
that three hundred dollars you gave Keith for Lee's
birthday? How do you know it wasn't spent on steroids
or some other pill? I bet they don't even know when
your birthday is. Then you bought that bitch flowers
when you saw her crying in the gym. Who else have you
helped? I'm sure there are others.

ME

(calmly)

Cynthia, none of these people asked for anything.

CYNTHIA

Cynthia pauses from packing and looks me straight in the eye.

Look, it's a beautiful trait that you help people. You
can't buy them happiness or the desire to better
themselves or the brains to recognize and appreciate the
wonderful qualities you have. If you are going to help
needy people, at least pick nice people—like me. And
that beautiful lady who doesn't see how beautiful she
really is. Back to me. Since you've got an open wallet,
how much can you give me toward a tummy tuck?
While you're paying, I might as well fix my droopy
eyelids.

ME

(whispering)

Your ass droops worse than your eyelids.

CYNTHIA

(laughing)

Then you'd better add it to the list. What did Ryan say?

ME

He reviewed the diet and the supplements, and he said the diet was for muscle growth and the vitamins were to sustain life. There were two items on the list he couldn't identify or find on the internet. He suggested asking the salesperson in the Vitamin Shoppe.

CYNTHIA

It's starting off bad already. My son may know about the supplements. What are they?

I pull the sheet out and point to the two items.

ME

Here.

CYNTHIA

This is blurry like it's been copied hundreds of times.

Cynthia holds the sheet alternating distances from her face in an attempt to read the writing.

I'm not sure of the letters.

Cynthia writes what she thinks the names are.

ME

So you need money to fix your vision too?

CYNTHIA

(laughing)

Come on, let's get out of here.

Cynthia and I leave her desk and head out via the long corridor.

ME

Tonight I'm stopping at the supermarket. The diet plan has me eating six or seven small, high-protein meals a day.

CYNTHIA

My son always cooked all the food for the week over the weekend. He'd put everything in ziplock bags and move them from freezer to refrigerator as necessary.

ME

That's a great idea.

CYNTHIA

Would you like to talk to him? I'm sure he can give you some pointers.

ME

Thanks, Cynthia, but the guys at the gym should be able to help me if Lee flakes out.

CYNTHIA

Hey, guess what? I met a guy last night. We had some great laughs.

ME

I'm keeping my fingers crossed for you, but not my legs.

CYNTHIA

Thanks. Better your fingers than your eyes.

ME

It's situational, Cynthia.

And so our new journeys began. Cynthia with her new man and me with my new project.

35 The First Training Session

Finally, the day arrived for the first training session. It was a Sunday. I arrived at the gym early and sat at the round table while I waited for Lee.

LEE

Did you get all the food and supplements?

ME

Yep, I'm right on schedule. Already had meal number one and meal number two.

LEE

Good. I just sent you an email. Your schedule is going to be:

- Twenty minutes of cardio twice a day; once in the morning before you eat, then once at night. You can count the boot camp as your p.m. cardio. You will not do cardio on leg day.

- Sunday is leg day.

- Do calves three days a week, never on consecutive days.

- Do abs four days a week. Abs are the one muscle group that you can do on consecutive days.

- We will pose Sunday after leg training and then Wednesday night after boot camp.

- Tuesdays and Thursdays we'll do upper body.

It is important that you eat on schedule. Plan to carry
a small cooler with the appropriate meals to wherever
you'll be.

ME

Okay.

Although it seemed like a lot of work, I figured I would still spend
less time at the gym than Victoria, who always seemed to be there.

LEE

Today we're doing legs.

Lee walks toward the leg press machine. As I follow Lee, I grab
sanitizing wipes from a sanitizing canister stand. Once at the leg press
machine, I wipe it down prior to sitting while Lee sets the weights.
Neal, the guy who claimed I was staring at him in the mirrors, was on
an adjacent machine.

NEAL

What? You're training him?

LEE

Yeah.

(to me)

Give me fifteen.

Lee adds more weight.

Fifteen more.

Lee adds even more weight.

Fifteen more.

Lee adds too much weight, and I struggle with the final fifteen reps.
This pattern of adding excessive weight continues on several more
machines, until I make a quick exit to the restroom.

Inside the men's restroom, vomiting sounds echo throughout the tiled
room. After washing my face, I return to the gym floor and find Lee
by the hack squat machine.

LEE

You okay?

ME

Yes.

LEE

Did you throw up?

ME

Yes.

LEE

Let's continue.

Using a sanitizing wipe I wipe off the hack squat machine as Lee puts the weights on it. To visualize the hack squat machine's motion, think of yourself with your back against a wall sliding up and down as you bend/straighten your legs. I position myself on the machine.

LEE

Keep flat-footed.

Fifteen reps. Ready. Go.

When I complete all the reps I stop for my minute break.

ME

I'm extremely dizzy. Give me another minute.

LEE

Okay.

Lee adds more weight.

Another fifteen.

I perform the repetitions and complain about being dizzy. During my minute break, Lee adds more weight, and I do the third set of fifteen repetitions. After a minute, Lee walks off to the next leg machine while I stay behind, holding on to the hack squat machine for several minutes with closed eyes, waiting for the dizziness to subside. This pattern on the hack squat machine will continue for several weeks.

At the leg curl machine.

LEE

You know the deal, fifteen.

Mid-repetition, I abruptly leave the machine and return to the restroom. Once again I hear my own vomiting sounds echo off the tiled walls. I wash my face, look into the washroom mirror, and shake my head no. I return to the gym floor to find Lee at the round table rather than at a machine.

ME

I was sick again.

LEE

Okay, that will be all for today.

So that was my first training session. It probably lasted thirty minutes at most. That first session should have been a warning about how the entire twelve weeks would go. Pavlov's dog probably caught on faster than I did.

36 The Second Training Session

As Sunday became Monday, I grew even more livid thinking about that first training session. There was no way I should have thrown up once—let alone twice. I arrived early for my second session and headed into the ab room where Martina, a younger gym member, was on a bench performing ab exercises. Martina grew up around bodybuilding and fitness, and she was a very nice person.

Inside the ab room.

ME

Can you show me some ab exercises? Lee said I need to do them four days a week.

MARTINA

Sure. Get on the other bench and follow along.

We do some ab exercises with me following Martina's lead. During our one-minute rest between sets, we talk.

ME

You've done shows before?

MARTINA

I've done a couple.

ME

Do I need to work out harder for a show than I would normally train?

MARTINA

No.

ME

Did you ever throw up while training?

MARTINA

Never.

ME

(shaking my head)

After twenty minutes it was time to start training with Lee.

Thanks for all your help.

MARTINA

Anytime you see me, you just come over and join in.

At the round table I find Lee sitting talking to his friends, Troy, Keith, and Ted. I walk over and stand next to him. Fueled by the conversation I had just had with Martina, my anger about Sunday's session is increasing to a new, dangerous level.

ME

(angrily)

You intentionally worked me hard to make me throw
up. I should not have thrown up twice. I'm paying you
to train me, not make me sick.

I storm off to a small room and start doing push-ups. When I notice Lee's shoes, I immediately stand up.

LEE

You made me look bad in front of my friends.

ME

(startled)

I apologize for making you look bad.

I was so upset I was shaking.

LEE

This is the way training goes. If you don't like it, you
shouldn't do the show. You should be glad to have me as
a trainer. Some people do a show without having an on-
site trainer and get their instructions by email or phone.
Having an on-site trainer is a help to you. Next time
you have a problem, we will discuss it together. Now,

if you want to continue to train for the show, you'll be
doing it my way. You have two minutes to decide.
ME
As Lee is talking, I am thinking, "What a bunch of shit."
Okay.
Lee walks off.

I have blown up at a few people in my lifetime. Usually I don't
because, quite frankly, most people or situations just aren't worth it.
Therefore, it appears that I don't stick up for myself. The fact of the
matter is I don't treat everything like it's life or death—certainly not
bodybuilding training. I was perplexed at my actions this time—a
bodybuilding contest wasn't going to make me or break me, so what
got me so agitated? I can tell you that I didn't deserve to be treated
that way. Although I am not proud to have blown up like that, I am
proud that I did not discount myself by keeping quiet like I usually
do. Still, I quickly realized that I needed to apologize for my behavior
just as Loretta would have done.

I find Lee's three friends who witnessed my tantrum together on
the gym floor. Keith is on the bench, Troy is spotting, and Ted is
watching.
ME
I need to apologize to each of you for exploding at Lee
in front of you. It was not very nice of me.
Nobody makes eye contact with me.
TED
It's cool.
Lee comes over.
LEE
You didn't have to do that.
ME
Yes, I did. If you're ready, I think my two minutes are
just about up.

Realizing that adding to someone's issues even as I was trying to help is unacceptable, I became very cautious not to discredit or upset Lee in any way after this incident. As a result, I kept my mouth shut regarding any failed training techniques and used my own resources (such as other gym members, videos, the internet) to compensate.

My method isn't without its drawbacks—very early during the body-building training I developed a lower leg twitch. I suspected it was the result of pent-up anger and disappointment acquired through the course of Lee's training. Initially lasting a few seconds, it gradually increased in duration until it was virtually nonstop.

37 Behind the Scenes

Looking at the daily diet plan with its six high-protein meals, I quickly realized it would be more efficient to do all the cooking for the week in one day, just as Cynthia had suggested.

Generally, I purchased food for the upcoming week on the preceding Friday or Saturday. From the diet Lee gave me, I created a shopping list to ensure I'd purchase everything at once. Typically, my cart was full of eggs, chicken, fish, Cream of Wheat, and low-carb vegetables. Eating healthy was incredibly expensive. Eventually, I learned that shopping at Costco significantly reduced my high food costs.

I purchased supplements once a month, again, in accordance with the plan Lee provided. Like the food, the supplements were also expensive.

I designated Sunday as my food-prepping day. Keep in mind that food preparation was in addition to the three hours I worked out. It was a massive effort (cooking, packaging food, and cleaning up), and eventually, over the first few weeks, I got the whole process down to just a couple of hours thanks to multitasking, good organization, and grilling the meat instead of baking, frying, or microwaving it.

The routine was:

- Position the grill outside the back door.

- Wash and place seven large whole sweet potatoes in a large bowl and microwave for twenty minutes.

- Boil four dozen eggs on the stove until hard boiled.

- Steam broccoli on the stove, and, when finished, drain in the sink using a colander.

- Prepare and grill seven chicken breasts and seven tuna steaks.

- Cook frozen string beans in the microwave.

- Cook frozen asparagus with the grilled meat.

- Bag supplements in packets to be consumed each morning, noon, and night.

- Portion food correctly by weight, place in meal containers, and refrigerate or freeze.

At the start of the third week, I was in the midst of the various stages of food preparation and cooking when I got the welcome distraction of a phone call.

Phone rings.

I put on my headset and pick up the dialer from the charger.

ME

Hello?

I put the dialer into my pocket, enabling me to move around the house.

JANICE

How have you been?

ME

Good. It's great to hear from you. You won't believe this: I'm doing a show.

JANICE

(startled)

What? Who's training you? Let me guess. Lee?

ME

Yep.

JANICE

How's it going?

ME

I'm not sure. I do have a couple of nagging questions I can't answer. Is it common to throw up during weight-lifting practice?

JANICE

No. Wait a minute … were you doing legs?

ME

Yes.

JANICE

Did you eat right before doing legs?

ME

Yes.

JANICE

You can't do that.

ME

I ate according to the schedule Lee gave me. He should know my eating schedule; he's my trainer. The other item I am concerned about is posing. I bought a posing video, which said to begin posing when you begin training. We posed for maybe a week, and then Lee canceled out several times.

JANICE

The video is right. You need to practice posing from the start of training, especially if you aren't familiar with the poses. You can look great and pose poorly, and the result will be a poor show finish. Or you can look okay, pose great, and finish well.

ME

Can Connor help me pose?

JANICE

Just a minute while I ask … Connor said he can't. He's

got baseball on the weekends, and he's too busy during the week. Sorry.

ME

I wish you hadn't left the gym. You and Connor are good people, and I trust you.

JANICE

If you have questions or need advice about what you're doing, just give us a call. I grew up around bodybuilding, and Connor's record is better than Lee's. We can tell you what you should be doing and where you should be at any point in the training.

ME

Thank you. I am going to take you up on your offer.

From that day forward, every Sunday while I was cooking, I talked to Janice. She and Connor became my surrogate coaches. They didn't have to, but they graciously did.

38 Strike the Pose

I had dieted successfully twice before, so I knew I had the stamina and endurance to do it a third time. I was also very comfortable working out either using the machines or the free weights. Posing, however, was totally foreign, and it made me very nervous. The poses seemed very unnatural and unmemorable. When was the last time you did a front lat spread? Do you even know what it is? It sounds dirty, doesn't it? On top of all that, for the first month of training, our posing practice was frequently canceled. It wasn't until the second month that we had consistent posing training on Wednesdays and Sundays.

The posing technique that Lee used was the "watch and do" technique. He imparted no insight regarding what the judges were looking for and no verbal instructions on how to execute the pose. I didn't find the "watch and do" technique effective. Since posing was new, I expected Lee to take things slowly and to explain each step. However, with Megan constantly deflating Lee's soul, I refused to criticize or complain to Lee about his training. Oddly enough, the posing video I bought also used the "watch and do" technique which validated Lee's method and therefore provided little value to me.

In the posing room. Lee is fully dressed with an oversize sports jersey top.

> LEE
> We will continue with the seven mandatory poses you will do in the show. Let's start with the front double biceps.

Lee demonstrates. Think of this as the "Popeye the Sailor Man" look, with both arms extended outward to the side and bent upward at the elbow with the closed fists near the ears.

LEE

Now you do it.

I try the pose. The look on Lee's face is telling me it's not good.

LEE

(in a mean voice)

No. Watch.

Lee demonstrates the pose again.

I try the pose again; I feel slightly more comfortable. Somehow instead of looking like Popeye, I look more like Olive Oyl poorly impersonating Popeye. Looking back now, I realize my elbows were probably lower than the horizon and not forward, so my chest and lats were not squeezed, and my wrists were not cocked down. But at the time I had no way of knowing what was wrong or right about what I was doing.

LEE

(sounding even meaner)

Use the mirrors to see that you are doing it right. Again.

I try again.

Instead of explaining what was wrong, Lee's voice just got progressively harsher—as though he were going to scare me into the perfect pose. It went on like this for a long time. But his tone was successful—successful in increasing the duration of my leg twitching.

39 Underdog Strikes Again

Like many others, I believe change is good. But when the change is the removal of eye candy, I have to put my foot down.

In the xCellFitness parking lot as I am walking toward the gym.

ME

Aren't you going the wrong way?

ZEKE

Just got kicked out of the gym. Some bullshit about stealing.

ME

Hell, Earl (the gym owner) claims that about everyone. I'll take care of it.

Inside the gym at the front counter.

ME

Earl, I'm glad you are here. I want to talk to you about Zeke.

EARL

I had to let him go—

ME

(cutting Earl off)

I don't care what Zeke did or allegedly did. With him gone I want to know who will provide the visual he did around here?

EARL

(acting puzzled)

What?

ME

Who is going to walk around with the big bulge in
front? You could do it, Earl, but you aren't here enough.
And you wouldn't need an extender.

The then gym manager, who was silently standing next to Earl, exited
immediately after I mentioned Zeke's big bulge. I suspect Earl, who was
always nice to me, found the whole conversation amusing and interesting.
Earl wasn't intimidated. Sadly, my argument didn't work. And no, nobody
ever replaced Zeke. Damn.

40 Ab Secret

I was in the kitchen washing the mountain of utensils, pots, pans, and plates required for my weekly food preparation. Talking to Janice made the phases of this laborious process pass by enjoyably. Today, like most times, I initiated the call.

On the phone in my kitchen.

ME

This show is costing me a fortune. To save some money, last week I bought the store-brand chicken. I was shocked at how much liquid was in the bowl after I microwaved it. They must have killed the chickens by drowning them. I'm switching back to the name brand.

JANICE

Yes, the expense is why Connor doesn't do shows yearly. Has Lee told you the secret to uncovering abs?

ME

What do you think?

JANICE

The trick is to rub Preparation H ointment on your stomach before going to bed. Then wrap yourself in plastic wrap so the oil doesn't ruin your bedding. Do your morning cardio before showering. With your diet and exercise regimen, you should see your abs in a couple of weeks.

ME

Preparation H, the stuff for hemorrhoids?

JANICE

Yeah.

ME

Lee mentioned that I would need to exfoliate just before tanning the night before the show. I didn't want to appear ignorant, so I just nodded my head. What does it mean? Sounds like something a parent whispers to his friends, "My son just *exfoliated* for the first time."

JANICE

It means you need to remove the dead skin on your body prior to tanning. The salesperson in the drugstore can help you find the right lotion or other items.

ME

Oh, thank God. I was going to stop at the adult store to inquire. How embarrassing that would have been.

41 Goodbye, Dear Friend

It started innocently enough. I was sitting in a conference room with several other coworkers eating the chicken in a bag, when my cell phone on the table vibrated. Not recognizing the number, I swiped the call to voice mail. This happened repeatedly within a few minutes.

My cell phone vibrates again.
COWORKER
> Someone is trying to get a hold of you. You'd better get
> it.

I grab the phone and put it up to my ear as I exit the conference room and enter the hallway.
ME
> Hello.

The tears roll down my face as I am told the news.

Several days later we are in a large room filled with pictures, flowers, and photo albums displayed on the various tables within a church. There is a picture of Tina with four other ladies in their youths. Various professional awards are prominently featured alongside the many photographs. The place is crowded with those whose lives have been touched by Tina. In the corner I see a group of Tina and Rich's family and friends. I make my way over to them. These are all people I know from the wonderful gatherings at their house.
TINA'S NEPHEW
> It's been a long time, Tom. How have you been?

ME

(shaking hands)

Yes, it has been a while. I am well, thanks. It's such a shame. Tina just turned sixty a few weeks ago.

TINA'S NEPHEW

(forgetting her birthday)

That's right. Aunt Tina's birthday is in September. I remember you from when I was a little kid.

ME

That's because I was always working at the house. And they were some of my fondest memories. Tina and Rich were such great influences during my teenage years. I learned to plan things out and do things the right way. And we certainly laughed a lot. Tina was a wonderful person. There have been many losers and questionable people in my life, but I am proud to know Tina and Rich and call them friends.

TINA'S NEPHEW

She fought so hard to live. Seventeen years of fighting. It's sad that the cancer won.

ME

I thought a miracle would happen. Maybe one did. But it doesn't seem that way to me right now.

TINA'S NEPHEW

I feel so bad I didn't see her before she passed.

ME

I just saw her a few weeks ago. I was shocked and saddened at how she had deteriorated, but it had never occurred to me until that day that she might not make it.

Minutes later we are inside the sanctuary area of the packed church. As I sit in the crowded pew, I place my unused tissues on my leg for quick access. The tears start immediately after I sit down.

At the podium, four of Tina's longtime friends are ready to speak. The first speaker starts.

TINA'S FRIEND

Tina called us her "fabulous four." I first met Tina …
I was too lost crying and grieving to comprehend the service. I'm sure it was beautiful. My tears didn't stop until the service ended. On my way out someone took one look at me and said I looked like a thunderstorm.

Tina was gone too early. I didn't feel that a miracle occurred that day. All these years later, it still doesn't feel that way.

42 Rules of Engagement

I will help just about anyone, but I do have participation parameters, also known as rules of engagement. I won't help someone who is unjustifiably or intentionally unkind toward me or others. Similarly, I won't help someone who is undermining my efforts. There were several times I felt Lee was exhibiting one or both of these behaviors. During those times, I temporarily halted all helping activities and acted indifferent to his issues, real or perceived, until his behavior improved.

Even though Lee didn't ask me to help him, I felt compelled to do so, and found I had another problem. Despite him asking to train me, after a few weeks he still didn't seem any more comfortable around me. How was I going to change that? I pondered the question for a few days and realized that in order to have any chance of success, I needed to recruit people Lee felt more comfortable with and let them help Lee too. This approach was tricky since the recruits had to be mature individuals whom I could trust. I had to trust that they would not tell Lee what I was doing, but in case they did, I wanted to appear as a casual participant and not the ringleader. Therefore, I would minimize my role by not having any involvement or knowledge of any recruit-initiated plans or activities, and only share the most basic information with them. After all, I reasoned that anyone else's participation was their business, not mine.

For two weeks I noted who Lee talked to, the depth of the conversation, and whether Lee seemed to value the other person's opinion. When I was confident that someone was a good candidate, I would pull him aside. My recruitment pitch went much like this:

To the prospective recruit:

ME

I've been working on a project to boost Lee's self-
esteem. I see you chatting with Lee quite a bit, and he
respects you. Can you help me with this?

ALEX

Sure, anything for Lee.

ME

You use any techniques you feel are correct. I won't ever
ask you about it or coordinate anything with you.

I pose the same question to Simon:

SIMON

For Lee, yes. Not for that Megan. She's a selfish bitch.

And to Judy:

JUDY

What do you mean, tell Lee that he's great?

Eventually, I recruited four people. I still continued my efforts, but only
when Lee acted in accordance with my rules of engagement. So, with five
people "helping" Lee, I expected to see results quickly and conclude P-Lee
shortly.

43 My Turn to Help

When you lift weights, you do several repetitions, maybe twelve or fifteen, without stopping. That makes a set. Typically, there is a one-minute break before starting the next set of repetitions. Often I spent my minute break walking around the gym. One quiet Sunday, when Lee was actually civil toward me, I resumed "Project Lee" after a hiatus due to Lee's poor behavior with pre-rehearsed, carefully selected words.

During the one-minute break between sets.

ME

Lee, have you ever noticed you don't have to be nice to people?

Lee seems puzzled but listens intently to what I am saying.

You don't have to buy people anything to get them to like you.

You don't have to be witty or funny.

You don't have to act a certain way for people to like you or want to be around you.

All you have to be ... is there!

You are a very lucky man.

Although he heard what I said, he did not respond. Since Lee does not publicly show much emotion, I didn't expect to see any, but I suspected he would think about it.

LEE

Give me fifteen more.

44 Problem Solved

It was Sunday, and I had completed my final set on the hack squat machine. As usual, I was feeling dizzy.

> ME
> (as I rest against the machine for support)
> We need to do something about this dizziness. This is at
> least the fifth straight week.

> LEE
> I think it's your breathing.

Immediately I realize Lee was right, I had not been using proper breathing techniques during exercise execution. I should have known, as Drew had warned me about my breathing during my new-member orientation. What I didn't understand is why Lee didn't correct this situation earlier.

> ME
> Thanks for pointing this out after all these weeks.

45 The Reality of Me

Every passing week, I saw little to no improvement in my posing. Still frustrated with the "watch and do" technique used in Lee's training and the posing video, I had to rethink my posing strategy. I recalled hearing that professional sports teams often record their practices to analyze player performance. So I figured perhaps if I recorded my posing sessions, I could study Lee's poses and his comments to determine what I was doing right and wrong. I purchased a video camera and tripod, which I had barely set up in the posing room when Lee entered.

LEE

What's all this?

ME

Well, since we only pose twice a week, and you want me to practice, I bought this camera. I think recording your demonstrations and comments will help me master the posing.

Lee walks off to the side and sits on the floor with his back against the wall. After I adjusted the tripod and camera, as usual, I took off my shirt to begin posing. We had missed several consecutive posing sessions, during which time Janice's suggested Preparation H technique had fully uncovered my abs by removing the water under the skin.

Lee notices my pronounced abs and appears stunned by them. I thought it is extremely odd that a longtime bodybuilder such as Lee is noticeably astonished to see abs appearing on someone preparing for a bodybuilding show. Did he think his diet plan and training wouldn't produce them? Perhaps it isn't very nice of me, but I didn't have the patience to deal with his astonishment. He can be shell-shocked on his time, not mine.

LEE

(in a trance from noticing my pronounced abs)
I'm going to make you a champion.

ME

I'm not doing this to be a champion.
After a few seconds, Lee breaks his trance.

LEE

Let's start with …
So I practiced for the usual forty-five minutes with each minute recorded on video.

Later that day, I am sitting in a kitchen chair to watch the recorded posing video. I push play on the remote. The video starts playing.

LEE

(kindly spoken)
Let's start with the side chest. It should look like this.
Lee demonstrates the pose. For the unfamiliar, consider what it would look like if you were walking on the sidewalk approaching someone perpendicular to you (such as facing the curb waiting for a bus), and they turned their body from the waist up toward you. There is specific a positioning of the arms and legs, but you get the basic idea.

LEE

Now you do it.
I try the side chest pose.

LEE

(calmly)
No, that's not quite it.
Lee effortlessly demonstrates the pose again.

I try the pose several times, and each time I am uncharacteristically told in a professional manner that my pose is not correct and to try again.

During the posing practice I grow enormously frustrated at the lack of progress, wasted money, and the failure of the multiple techniques I tried to improve my posing. I start complaining, which is fully captured on video.

ME

(frustrated, waving hands, and speaking in a high voice)
We've been doing this for weeks, and I'm not getting
any better. It can't be this hard—college physics was
easier than this. Something is wrong.

"Shocked," "horrified," and "embarrassed" are the three words that best describe my reaction to viewing myself in the video. Seeing and hearing my high, faggy voice and effeminate gestures, I realized this must be the real me and how others see me. Perhaps that is why Lee didn't provide details on what I was doing wrong. How do you politely or professionally tell someone to be more masculine? Will the show audience see a bodybuilder or a showgirl? The reality of me and its potential consequences is too much to take.

Using the remote control, I turn off the video.

ME

(mumbling)
Some "natural." A natural fool.

Never watching the video again was the easy part. The much harder part is pondering the questions like, "Is this the me others see? Is this why I am alone?" That's not the me that I see. I knew I didn't have the time, energy, or mentality to deal with *me* until sometime after the show.

I watched the video long enough to make a second interesting observation. When being recorded, Lee was less mean toward me during my flawed poses. This couldn't be coincidental. So I got to thinking: Would

Lee be nicer toward me, or at least more professional, if I brought someone with me into the posing sessions? Soon *another* new posing plan would be created.

46 Dark Moments

I was feeling melancholy. Seeing myself on the video greatly contributed to the condition, along with feelings of loneliness. Cynthia had suggested we meet at the mall one Saturday evening. Hell, I would have met her on the moon.

Inside Abercrombie & Fitch with music playing in the background. I hold a shirt up to my nose.

ME

I think they must spray cologne on their shirts.

CYNTHIA

Oh, they do. Listen, I need you to make me a promise.
If I'm ever in a coma, and my kids are deciding whether
or not to pull the plug, play this music. If I respond
with even the slightest movement, don't yank the chord.

ME

No problem. But if you're covered in sheets and a
hospital gown, we may miss the movement. We need
another sign. How about farting? You're good at that.

CYNTHIA

Well, if I fart, and you see movement, set the dinner
table because mama's coming home!

ME

Do you see anything your son would like?

CYNTHIA

Not sure yet. I like how these shirts have an athletic fit.

Cynthia pauses and looks right into my eyes from across the rack.
Don't even think about buying Lee one.
ME
Don't worry about that. Can't afford it. This show is
costing me a fortune.
CYNTHIA
Hey, I saw in the paper that the nursery manager near
your house committed suicide.
ME
I heard. His cancer came back, and he didn't want to go
through treatment again. Can't blame him.
CYNTHIA
Me either. But it's so sad when someone feels there is
no other option than suicide. Fortunately, I have never
personally known anyone who did it.
ME
When I lived in Raleigh, I dated a guy named Joey.
He was forty-two and I was twenty-seven. Joey was an
overly nice guy. He lived in Raleigh all his life and knew
everyone. And I mean everyone. And everyone liked
him. He was very witty. Joey was the first person you'd
call if you needed something. Sadly, he was the last one
invited to a party.

He once told me a story I found upsetting: A group of
guys were going on a trip, and he was not initially asked
to go. Apparently, all four guys were sharing the same
room, and one of them had to drop out … taking his
money with him. So they asked Joey, and he went. He
excitedly told me what a wonderful time he had. I asked
him why he accepted the invitation when they were
only interested in his money.
Cynthia sensed a seriousness in this story and paused shopping to

focus on what I was saying. I was in a haze as I looked through the clothes while talking.

ME

(slowly moving from rack to rack)

Joey said, "But I got to go."

Joey and I dated for months but it was a difficult relationship. He didn't understand why I worked so much. Plus, my friend Richard from work was in the advanced stages of AIDS. Richard was a genius and, like Joey, fun to be around. Joey didn't understand why I spent so much time with Richard or did things for Richard. I guess Joey had seen so many friends die of AIDS, he was hardened to the compassion of it all.

Joey was desperately seeking a partner and fell hard for me. He had been so lonely. He'd say, "Tom, if this isn't real, you've got to tell me." I said nothing … nothing every time. I knew Joey was in trouble and that breaking up with him was going to hurt him. But I did absolutely nothing to help him.

I didn't mean to mislead him. I was barely coping with my own issues, and I couldn't deal with his issues too.

I transferred to Connecticut, and shortly after I got there, one Wednesday night, I received a landline call from my friend Steve in North Carolina. Speaking rapidly and matter-of-factly, Steve said, "Tom, Joey committed suicide. The funeral is Saturday. Are you coming? You should—you were his last."

I was speechless. Steve went on to say that Joey

committed suicide by hanging himself from a light fixture at the top of the second-floor stairwell.

I was so shocked that, after we hung up, I called Steve back just to confirm he had called. We reviewed the details, and I barely comprehended the sad reality of the situation.

When I got in bed that night I smelled Joey next to me. The next night I smelled him again. Finally, on the third night, the night before his funeral, I couldn't take the smell any longer and yelled out, "Joey, go to heaven." Immediately the smell left and never returned.

Joey didn't deserve any of that. He was a great, substantial guy in character, morals, and vocation. Joey's tragedy has impacted me in every relationship I've had since. I think about him often. I try to take on his best qualities of being polite and helpful. Of course, I get the rest of my great attributes from my heroes, Loretta Lynn and Mother Teresa.

Cynthia catches the humor amid the seriousness.

Remembering Joey, I try to help people in trouble or potential trouble; I don't want to live through another senseless suicide. If someone mistreats me, I lose sleep for a night or two. At worst case, I take off a day from work. But if I mistreat someone, I lose sleep for a week. And you know how bad my normal sleep is.

CYNTHIA

You can't blame yourself. You aren't a doctor. You didn't know he was going to commit suicide.

ME

No, but I knew he was in trouble. To me, if you know or suspect someone is in trouble, and you don't act on it, you are guilty. It serves me right that I can't find a partner. When I actually found someone who was a good-natured and stable guy, I didn't appreciate him. They say good guys finish last. Now I realize they finish first.

CYNTHIA

Nice guys do finish first, but don't let people take advantage of your good nature.

ME

They can only for so long until I get tired of it. I have issues spending money on myself, so you'd better believe I count every cent I spend on other people. Why am I always the one who can see the potential in others?

CYNTHIA

Look, if they can't see their potential, it isn't up to you to draw it out of them. Who says we need to live up to our potential? Maybe some people are happy with complacency and mediocrity. Who says people should live according to your expectations and the potential you see? These people aren't kids, they're adults. If they have issues, they need to learn the skills to solve them. They can write to Dear Abby. And she'll reply to them *after* she responds to me.

ME

Life is simple. The answers are in the classic country music I listen to. Look, I know I won't get a trophy or a better place in heaven. I don't want the time or money back that I invest in people. Most of the time, they don't even realize what I am up to, so I certainly don't expect a thank you. But it gives me great satisfaction knowing that I tried to help someone.

CYNTHIA

How are their issues your problem?

ME

Cynthia, I appreciate you telling me all this. Someone
has to. And maybe one day I'll realize I've been one
big fool. But my actions are from the heart, and I'll
continue with them until something or someone makes
me see it differently. Then I will just move on. I just
can't afford to deal with the guilt from another death.

CYNTHIA

Are you sure you aren't running away from your own
problems by engrossing yourself in other people's
perceived problems?

ME

Perhaps. I've started a little policy you'll be happy
to hear. After I help someone, I reward myself with
something. That way I am spending money on myself.

Joey deserved so much better than he got, and he deserves to be remembered. I heard that Joey's passing woke people up about their treatment of others. I hope that is true.

Joey has been dead for many years now, and one favorite memory comes to mind. We were visiting Joey's friend and sitting around the living room. The friend, with a foot crossed on his knee, said, "Wouldn't it be great if your dick was the length of your foot?" Without missing a beat Joey said, "At what age?"

Everybody laughed. Rest in peace, Joey.

47 Sunday's Family Spaghetti Dinner

Prior to leaving the gym, Drew handed out a sheet of paper with his contact information and an open invitation to his Sunday family spaghetti dinner. I found the paper while looking through the stash of car magazines I kept between the front seats in my car. Vanessa agreed to go with me, and I emailed Drew. Keep in mind that I was still in training, so I took my own food—chicken in a bag.

Drew, Vanessa, and I are seated around the table inside Drew's house after dinner. Everyone else is either cleaning up or in the family room.

> ME
>
> Drew, I miss you at the gym. I wish you'd return.
>
> DREW
>
> My business is going great. After years of driving to meet clients, they are coming to me. Nothing is better than working from home. A few months ago, I picked up a client you know, Dawn.
>
> ME
>
> I haven't seen her in a long time, so I assumed she left the gym. Ah, I use to tell Dawn that Lee was a great trainer. In fact, after you left, I went around the gym telling all your former clients they should use Lee.
>
> DREW
>
> Lee was so rough with her that she would cry after the workouts. That's when she came to me.

ME

Dawn is a nice person. She didn't deserve that. Now I
feel like such a fool for recommending him.

DREW

Would you recommend him now based on your
experience?

I hated to say it, perhaps because I hate to be wrong, but I shook my head
no.

48 Graduating to "After-Photo" Status

I did not notice the weight loss occurring, but I knew it was, since my clothes weren't fitting. I'd rather be in outdated fashions than wearing clothes that don't fit. It's not like I could buy new clothes every month. Out of necessity, I formulated a trick that worked quite well. For my pants, I slid my front and rear belt loops toward my hips, which placed the extra material at my side. Not only did my pants appear to fit, but this trick had the added bonus of accentuating both my basket and ass. I couldn't have been happier.

Another, more interesting circumstance related to my weight loss was developing. Others started noticing my improved appearance, and I was greatly amused by their reactions. Of the several stories occurring at this time, this is my favorite. I consider this event as achieving "after-photo" status.

In the gas station convenience store where for years I have purchased lottery tickets.

ME

Two Powerball tickets, please.

I give the guy a ten-dollar bill. The familiar male store clerk makes change that oddly includes coins along with paper currency. As he places the coins in my palm, the clerk rubs my palm in an obvious, prolonged way. I ignore it as I put the money in my pocket.

Realizing I am thirsty, I get a bottle of water and place it on the counter.

The same store clerk wraps his fist around the water bottle and slowly runs it down the length of the bottle as I dig out the money from my pocket to pay for it. I just pretend I don't notice what he is doing.

There is that old saying about being careful what you wish for because it could come true. Well, once I had reached "after-photo" status, although I felt and acted the same, I couldn't believe how people reacted toward me, like that store clerk. I wouldn't treat anyone like that. Overall, I found it more entertaining to be the dreamer than the dream.

49 Prepping for the Show

Eventually, the highly regimented weeks brought us closer to the show date, and it was time to start show planning.

> LEE
> I need to change your diet plan. Follow this from now on.

Lee hands me a piece of paper.

> ME
> I hope this is better than the last one. That plan specified items on the grocery list that weren't synchronized with the daily ration. It was a good thing I reviewed it prior to going to the store; I spent at least an hour figuring out what I needed to actually purchase.

> LEE
> You need to order posing trunks. There are several online sites you can use. Get a size thirty waist and whatever color you want. Some guys buy two different colors so they will look like different contestants to the judges during each appearance. You are also going to need a song to pose to.

> ME
> Brian suggested I pose to a song called "Warrior."

> LEE
> Okay.

ME

Are you going with me to Hartford?

For a split second Lee's face loses composure as though going to
Hartford or potentially sleeping in the same room with me was not
something he wanted or thought about doing.

ME

(continuing without a delay)

If so, I will get you a hotel room and a trainer's pass.

Lee's facial composure resumes.

LEE

That's fine.

And so I made the necessary changes—diet adjustments, posing trunk purchase, and arrangements for Lee to attend the show. Like with homeownership, the money continued to fly out of my wallet.

50 Paving the Way

I had several male friends who realized, while they were married to women, that they were gay—and maybe, since the rumors persisted, Lee fell into that category.

One good thing about living in a small city is everybody knows someone who knows someone else. I had heard that Lee's father, Luther, worked in a local appliance store. As fate would have it, I have an older friend, Helen, who works in the same store. Helen has sold me many appliances, so whenever I am in the store I make it a point to visit and chat with her. It never takes long for our chats to turn to laughter. I figured perhaps, with Helen's help, I could smooth out the road for Lee should he actually be gay without ever mentioning or implying it to his father.

Helen looks up from her desk in the appliance section.

HELEN

Hey stranger, what brings you in here?

ME

I need water filters. Changing them is the absolute
worst. Even with pressing that pressure release button, a
massive effort is required to remove the canister.

HELEN

Honey, did you read the instructions? Probably not,
because there wasn't a picture of a good-looking guy in
them. After you shut off the main water line, open a
faucet prior to pressing the pressure button.

ME

Ah. Yes, that'll do it. Hey, I was told my trainer's father works at one of these stores. Does anyone you know have a bodybuilder son by the name of Lee?

HELEN

Oh, you're referring to Luther's son. Lee lives in his basement.

ME

Yes, that's right. I need you to do me a favor. When you have a minute with Luther, make up some fictitious male relative who just discovered that he is gay and needs to divorce his wife.

HELEN

Is that what happened between Lee and his wife?

ME

I don't know. But I want to plant the idea in Luther's head that it's a common occurrence—just in case.

HELEN

Got it, sweetie.

ME

How are you doing these days?

HELEN

Oh, my knees need to be replaced. The left knee will be this year, and the right knee next year.

ME

Don't worry, Helen. You'll be back to giving blow jobs in no time. Did you need me to fill in during your recovery? But you know, a bird in the crack beats two in the hands!

51 From Bad to Worse

I didn't think things could get worse, but they did. I felt I was giving 1,000 percent as a trainee, while my trainer was giving maybe 25 percent. Lee texted me he had surgery and was unable to train me that night! I was livid. Lee had an older client, Simon, who trained prior to me. When I arrived at the gym, I searched for Simon to ask him what he knew about the surgery.

On the gym floor.

ME

Did you train with Lee today?

SIMON

No, he had surgery.

ME

Yes, he texted me about two hours ago. Was the surgery scheduled in advance?

SIMON

Yes, I even offered to take the day off from work to be with him at the hospital, but his parents took him instead.

ME

What's the recovery period?

SIMON

Six weeks.

ME

Great. I'm going to have to do this by myself. Like I've always said, in life you've got to figure out everything for yourself—everything except for sex. And there are plenty of people willing to show you that.

SIMON

Tom, who showed you?

After my solo workout, I headed to the posing room to practice by myself. Quite surprisingly, Neal came into the room. Neal is the guy who, on that first training session with Lee, questioned Lee about him training me.

ME

I just realized the twins are your sisters. They are beautiful. If you had been born female, you'd be quite a looker!

NEAL

(laughing)

Tom, I'll be teaching you to pose while Lee is recovering. Let's start.

ME

Did Lee ask you to help, or are you volunteering?

NEAL

No, he did not ask me. Let's see you do a front lat spread.

I do the front lat spread pose. Professional bodybuilders and trainers please forgive me for this description, but think of it as the hands on the hip "where the hell have you been" look someone gives you when you've been missing in action.

NEAL

It isn't right. Again.

Neal didn't explain what was wrong. I repeated the pose.

NEAL

It isn't right. Again.

Until Lee returned to the gym, several gym members tried to teach me to pose. I appreciated their effort; however, they used the dreaded "watch and do" method. Finally, Peter showed up with a training technique that met my expectations.

PETER

Take off your shirt and roll up your shorts.

Much to my shock, Peter also removes his shirt and rolls up his shorts.

PETER

Now we are going to do the front lat spread.

I fully expected the "watch and do" method that everyone else used.

> The important thing to understand is these poses are designed to allow the judges to see the entire physique by highlighting multiple muscles within one pose— more than just the muscles in the name of the pose. The judges look for the definition, presentation, symmetry, and muscularity of your physique. And you will have to perform each pose quickly and at different angles so that all of the judges can see you regardless of where they sit and where you stand.

Peter demonstrates the multiple angles needed for the judges to see the contestants.

I try.

Peter walks over and points out what is wrong while I am posing.

PETER

> You will look fuller and bigger by not shrugging your shoulders during the pose. You will want to show off your abs, so let's see you crunch them. During the show you may be oily, and your hands may start slipping down your waist.

I stop posing to watch Peter demonstrate.

PETER

> So you may want to start with downward-facing palms and hook your thumb around your waist, then push your fists into your body.

The look on Peter's face tells me I have succeeded with a near-perfect pose! The smile on my face reflects a ray of hope this show won't be a total embarrassment.

Forty minutes later, the posing practice ends with me having a renewed optimism.

                              ME
          Can you please be my posing instructor?
                            PETER
          Sorry, I just don't have the time to commit.
                              ME
          Peter, thank you so much. You've given me hope that I
          can pull this show off.
                            PETER
          You're welcome. If you see me here and you need help,
              just come get me.
Peter exits.

I have just finished putting on my shirt and shoes when Rod enters the room. Rod is the guy that Victoria craves. And rightly so, for Rod is an attractive man. I walk over to Rod, who just finished a set of crunches and is taking a one-minute break.

                              ME
          Rod, I know you are dating Megan, but what about a
          lady like Victoria? She's a good person, good natured, a
          great mother, and she'd do anything to please you. Don't
          go for the beauty queens and hope they'll have half the
          qualities that Victoria has.
Then Rod spoke those golden words that still bring a smile on my face:

                             ROD
          Tom, there ain't no beauty queens here!
Yep, he really said that. I almost fell over laughing.

Lee's recovery may have been six weeks, but with an arm in a sling, he returned to train me after several days. I didn't know what the sling meant for my training, specifically his weight lifting spotting ability and posing instruction—I just kept quiet and didn't ask. For at least the first week that Lee was back at the gym, people came over during my training to inquire as to the nature of his sling, the injury, and the recovery. Since he had been a gym member for more than fifteen years, I was impressed by the number of people who stopped to talk to him. Even though a trainer should focus solely on his client, I viewed their concern as a wonderful expression of love, and perhaps Lee would recognize it as such. His doing so would facilitate a successful project ending. I marveled at the prospect of how human nature and timing could organically aid in Lee's project. It was wishful thinking. Deep inside I realized I was just making up an excuse for his frequent distractions during my paid training sessions.

52 Mirror, Mirror

All of that cardio did have one big benefit besides making me look great. It gave me forty minutes a day to use the mirrors to watch, stalk, stare, or whatever you want to call it. By now I had my technique perfected. Watching the attractive, hulking, muscular guys turned the boring cardio into fun, and the minutes flew by. I couldn't wait to do cardio!

Judy and I are on adjacent treadmills chatting away while our eyes, aided by the mirrors, are focused on the attractive, muscular African American men working out.

JUDY

Aren't they hot?

ME

Oh yeah. With any of them, my legs would be in the air faster than the launching of Sputnik.

JUDY

If I weren't in a relationship, I'd be making a move on those guys. Can you believe some people have a hang-up over me dating black men?

ME

(surprised)

What, a hang-up in this day and time? Well, the way I see it is we're all the same color in the dark. Come to think of it, the only bad balls I've had were printed on lottery tickets.

JUDY

Have you ever invited strangers over?

ME

Sometimes. One time, in the middle of the night, the guy says, "Do you believe in God?" I said, "Why, am I going to see Him sooner rather than later?"

JUDY

You are crazy.

ME

Well, it's not like my address is written on all the men's room walls. First I have to see the guys locally on the internet for several weeks, so they just aren't passing by. Then I need a phone number and some texts to make sure they are legit.

JUDY

But what if they show up not looking like their picture?

ME

It happens. I tell them we can't have sex because I just ate sauerkraut.

Surprisingly, one of the hulking men jumps. His front, waist-level clothing's jiggle is obvious. Judy and I simultaneously lose our footing and nearly fall off our treadmills. It is very ungraceful but hilarious. Fortunately, neither of us is hurt, and thankfully nobody ever questions what happened.

After the cardio, I head to my car in the parking lot and get in. Busy reading my cell phone messages, I didn't notice that Neal had walked up to my car window.

Neal taps several times on my window.

I put the window down.

ME

(startled)

What's up, Neal?

NEAL

Can you loan me twenty dollars? Things are really tight
right now.

I reach for my wallet.

ME

You haven't repaid me the forty you already owe me.
Here.

I hand Neal a twenty through the window.

NEAL

Thanks, man.

53 Another Recruitment

Every weekday for twelve weeks, I dragged myself out of bed at 5:00 a.m. and headed to xCellFitness for my morning cardio. Typically, I did morning cardio by myself, but with the aid of my country music heroes who'd sing me into consciousness.

At 5:30 a.m. the inside of the gym is dimly lit. There are a few early birds scattered around aided by one employee/trainer. Half-asleep, I keep to myself, but I notice the other members are quite social, especially the two older ladies on the equipment behind me. Sometimes they talked so loud, they drowned out the music from my earbuds.

On this morning I had invited Judy to join me for cardio. After the workout, Judy and I are wiping down our treadmills.

JUDY

You have to get up early for twelve weeks? This isn't for me.

ME

It's not so bad after you get used to it.

JUDY

I don't know how you can train with Lee. Lee always looks so disconnected while he trains you.

ME

I've offered to pay other people, but I can't get anyone. I don't understand why.

JUDY

That's because you are Lee's client.

ME

Ah, so that's why.

Cheryl comes over.

ME

Here you go. All cleaned.

I was hoping you were coming this morning.

CHERYL

Like it or not, I'm here.

Cheryl gets on the machine and starts programming it while I am talking. We are still conversing as her treadmill belt starts moving.

ME

I need a favor. I've been working on a project to boost
Lee's self-esteem. I've recruited various people. He
has an issue with being around me. When you are
available, could you come to my posing sessions Sunday
midmorning and Wednesday night?

CHERYL

No problem. Lee used to hang around with me and my
boyfriend; he'll be cool with me.

54 Opposing Views

On the phone during my Sunday food preparation.

JANICE

How's the posing going?

ME

We resumed, but since I missed weeks of practice,
posing only twice a week isn't going to be enough.

JANICE

You'd better find someone.

ME

Has Connor's schedule let up enough to help me out?

JANICE

I'll ask ... No, Connor is still too busy.

ME

I've asked Cheryl to sit in on the posing so that Lee
will be more comfortable around me and not so mean.
Perhaps he'll work harder at correcting my poor posing.

JANICE

How do you feel about your abs and calves? They are
the two most difficult muscle groups to develop.

ME

I think they'll be fine. But I'm worried about my pecs.

JANICE

Pecs.

(a few seconds later)

Connor says to increase the dumbbell flies and close-grip weighted push-ups for pecs.

ME

I'm already spending three hours a day, every day, at the gym. This will increase that time.

JANICE

Well, Connor's record is better than Lee's. If you want to improve, you'll need to do what Connor says.

ME

Is it common to have body parts twitching as a result of this training?

JANICE

What do you mean?

ME

I've had twitches in my lower leg since the beginning of this training. Now one of my eyelids has started twitching. I'm not sure if it's the result of the increased caffeine, increased stress, or both.

JANICE

Never heard of anyone ever having that issue, so I doubt if it's a result of the training. You'd better get it checked out by a doctor.

I never went to the doctor as Janice suggested. Like the leg twitching, the eyelid twitching increased in duration as the training continued. Regardless of its source, I knew it wasn't a good sign. So I decided I needed something joyful to look forward to and a means to end the stress and body twitching. It was time to invest in myself as I do in other people.

I found a sixteen-day transatlantic cruise departing immediately after my show and at the start of my anticipated recovery from the show embarrassment. If nothing else, taking a trip would force me to socialize when all I would want to do is hide and feed my anger upon reflection over Lee's poor treatment and training. Despite the fact that this bodybuilding show was costing me a fortune, I hated to spend one cent on a vacation. But I needed to end the twitching before it morphed into something worse. So it was easy to justify the trip's expense. I booked the cheapest priced cabin down by the coal bins. After all the hours spent daily to train and prepare for the show, having one full day just to pack for the trip seemed very excessive.

In addition to strictly adhering to Lee's training regimen, I followed Janice and Connor's bodybuilding suggestions fully. It wasn't easy. I was very tired from getting up early and getting to bed late. Keep in mind that I maintained a full day at work plus all my additional chores (house cleaning, lawn work, laundry) along with the required daily training hours.

55 A True Miracle

As anticipated, Cheryl's presence during my posing sessions reduced Lee's often harsh vocal delivery during training. What wasn't anticipated was Megan and her girls started appearing in the posing room when we were there. This was no coincidence. And they would harass poor Cheryl.

Cheryl and I are walking out of the posing room. In the distance I spot a guy who looks vaguely familiar.

CHERYL

(to me)

Megan and her girls are intentionally in my face when I am with you. They have the whole big room, so why do they need to be around me?

I shrug my shoulders, but I know that Megan doesn't want any females honing in on Lee. It was as if, since Megan couldn't have him, no other woman should.

CHERYL

You know what you need? A simulated bodybuilding show walk-through so you know what to expect.

ME

I've already asked but it fell on deaf ears. Coming from you, it will show that it's obvious to an outsider. In case that doesn't work, I ordered a show video.

The guy I first noticed when Cheryl and I left the posing room is heading directly toward us. He seems so familiar I think I recognize him from when I first joined the gym. I stop the guy when we are within speaking distance.

ME

Excuse me. There use to be a guy here with serious mobility issues and a service dog. He would exercise the dog on a treadmill.

JOSH

That was me.

CHERYL

I remember you. You look great.

JOSH

Thanks. I got messed up in the Middle East. After several operations and lots of rehab and hard work, here I am, good as new. I had great doctors and therapists.

ME

Congratulations. How inspiring. Stories like yours never seem to conclude this way.

JOSH

Thank you.

CHERYL

Where's the service dog?

JOSH

Home with my grandparents.

The difference in Josh's mobility was amazing. If I hadn't seen him before the surgeries, I'd never believe it was the same person.

56 A Revelation about My Heroes and Me

Even following the bland bodybuilding diet, lunch is still the highlight of my day. Fortunately, much to my delight, I was allowed to use Tabasco to improve the dull-tasting food. I put Tabasco on just about everything—and still do. I'd probably eat cardboard coated with it! By this time I ate so much fish that when I saw a river, I felt the urge to spawn!

Cynthia and I are best buds and comfortable enough to share our innermost feelings and beliefs. Seated alone in a corner of the cafeteria with Cynthia.

ME

I realized something startling a few years ago. Loretta Lynn has the equivalent of a fourth-grade education. But she became a superstar following the basic values her parents taught her: to work hard, be honest, and treat others well.

CYNTHIA

I think she had a little talent, and her husband gets a lot of credit too.

ME

So if Loretta Lynn, the poor housewife, stopped me on the street, I would give her the bum's rush. But if I suspected Loretta Lynn, the entertainer, was in a fifty-mile radius, I'd hunt her down like a heat-seeking missile. What perplexes me is why I wouldn't want anything to do with her at a different point in her life.

She's the same person, whether rich or poor, famous or not. So that's why I am nice to everyone; you just never know who is the next Loretta Lynn.

CYNTHIA

Referring to those who Cynthia feels are only after my money and good heart.

These people ain't no Loretta Lynn. And they ain't Thomas Caesar either.

ME

You never know. My heroes are druggies, illiterates, and jailbirds. You know them as some of country music's biggest stars. I finally realized that, after a childhood of being on the losing end of comparisons with my mother's friends' kids, I am the only person I have to live with until I die. I am not perfect, but I am the subject matter expert on myself. I am a good person with good intentions. I am pleased with the way I turned out. If I don't love me, I can't expect or ask anyone else to. I love me.

CYNTHIA

And you should. There is a lot to love. Of course we need to blame our parents. It was the way we were brought up, to be considerate and thoughtful of others. It's important, but what happens is we discount ourselves in the process. We put others' needs ahead of our own, and often people today can't or won't reciprocate.

ME

It's society. You know, it's so sad that people feel the need to conform to what the media says we need to look like and how we need to act, speak, or dress. They force unrealistic expectations onto us. Most of the time someone is just trying to sell some worthless product.

Growing up, I'd hear Loretta Lynn say in interviews how hard it was to just be herself. What she was saying was not to be a copy but instead be an original. She was encouraging us to embrace ourselves. What a concept!

CYNTHIA

Today you're better off treating people like they treat you or just ignoring them. Whichever is easier for you.

57 Did You Hear?

Why is it when someone says, "Did you hear …" what follows is seldom good? When Brian said he was going to meet up with the "old party group," I knew bad news would eventually follow.

One night, there were several xCellFitness workers gathered around the front counter when I entered. While I was scanning my identification, one of the gym workers broke from the group and came over to me.

FRONT COUNTER WORKER

Did you hear?

ME

Hear what?

FRONT COUNTER WORKER

Brian was arrested for exposing himself.

ME

(doubting)
Really? How did you hear?

FRONT COUNTER WORKER

It was in the paper.

ME

What did it say?

FRONT COUNTER WORKER

He was in his car by the university and asked female students for directions. When they got close to his car, he exposed himself.

ME

(surprised)

He exposed himself while seated in the car?

FRONT COUNTER WORKER

Yes.

ME

With what? A pelvic thrust?

I lean inward to the counter to make my point.

How far did she have to lean into the car before she saw something?

The gym worker laughs loudly.

Was he wearing his extender?

The gym worker is in a state of hysterics.

If he wanted to flash someone, he could have just called me or Judy.

Shaking my head, I walk away, mumbling:

There goes a grand down the toilet.

My comments spread like wildfire around the gym. I heard Brian didn't think they were funny.

That event taught me a very important lesson about helping people. Sometimes external factors, which you have little or no control over, may negatively impact your project. They're not your fault, and they can jeopardize your current and future efforts. Be prepared for external factors and don't take them personally when they occur.

Disappointment aside, I still had to work out, so I walked over to the elliptical area. I secured the machine next to Victoria by hanging my workout gloves over the control panel and placing my one-gallon water bottle on the floor. As I set my cardio workout parameters, I could see that Victoria had been on her machine a long time and was probably almost finished with her cardio session.

VICTORIA

I know, I know. Everyone is beautiful in their own way.

ME

I don't know about everyone, but I know about you.
You are beautiful in every way.

VICTORIA

They're all laughing at me. I am so fat and ugly. Megan
is the only one telling me the truth. She says I'm not
that bad.

Victoria turns around and looks in the mirror; when she sees her
reflection, a pained look crosses her face, and she makes a hissing
sound.

ME

If anyone is laughing at you, it's because you're listening
to Megan. We all know she only wants your money.
If she told you that you looked good, there would be
no need to train you. Victoria, I'm worried about you.
Have you seen a doctor lately?

VICTORIA

My doctor wants me to attend all-day therapy sessions
for one solid month instead of once a week.

ME

Sounds like a great idea.

VICTORIA

I can't do it.

ME

Why?

VICTORIA

I need to work.

ME

If you did the program he wants, how much income
would you lose?

VICTORIA

(hesitates to think about it)
About eight hundred and fifty dollars.

ME

Look, I'll give you the eight hundred and fifty dollars.
But you've got to promise to attend the therapy every
day.

VICTORIA

That is so sweet of you. My doctor should be finishing
up his night session. I'll call him in a couple of minutes.

Consequently, Brian went into isolation due to the exposure incident. He
disappeared from both the bar and the gym. Naturally, there were all kinds
of rumors. Once in a while Barbara would mention how Brian was doing,
but I never inquired about him or asked for more details beyond what information she volunteered.

58 Karma's a Piss

I was fortunate that Equilibrium featured a full food menu with healthy food options, so I could socialize without ruining my diet. I loved the way Equilibrium's cook prepared my big salad of iceberg lettuce, tomatoes, and chicken breast. The compliments regarding my body's transformation were a common occurrence from my friends.

On the other end of the bar, Arnold and Randall were being loud and obnoxious as they argued over vacation plans. Randall was already drunk and belligerent. They acted like a married couple who had been together one day too long. Arnold tried to maintain some decorum. Four of the six bartender's shot glasses along the back bar wall were empty.

Seated with Arnold at the bar, Randall is loud and slurring his words.

RANDALL

I think we should vacation in Las Vegas.

ARNOLD

We already talked about this, Randall. We are going to Key West.

RANDALL

We need to vacation in spots we're considering for retirement. We can't afford to retire in Key West. Even if we could, it's too far from Miami for major medical services.

ARNOLD

I know, Randall, but there's no ocean in Las Vegas. I read in the Sunday edition of the *New York Times* how living near the ocean has a very calming, healing effect on people.

RANDALL

Then the ocean will need to heal you if your vertigo acts up. *I'm* not driving you to Miami for treatment.

I am seated a few seats away. Lyle is with me, and both of us are ignoring Randall and Arnold.

LYLE

When they go on vacation, we're all on vacation. When is your show?

ME

In another month.

LYLE

You really look great.

ME

Thanks. Funny how the gym guys think training for a show is tough. Eight weeks into it, it isn't tough. Tough is showing yourself against the accepted norm and opening yourself to ridicule, humiliation, and harm just to satisfy an inner desire. Now that's tough.

RANDALL

(spoken like a directive rather than a request and loud enough to be heard from several feet away)
Lyle, another one.

ARNOLD

How many is that?

RANDALL

It's only my third.

LYLE

(loudly)
Coming right up.
(whispering softly to me)
Tough is putting up with the two of them!
(leaning in toward me)

It happened. A bartender pissed in their drinks.
(leaning outward, no longer whispering but smiling)
Lemonade anyone?
I lean forward toward Lyle.

                    ME

(in a whisper)
God, wouldn't they just shit if they knew someone
pissed in their drink!
While Lyle and I are talking, a young gay couple enters. I recognize
them. Lyle leaves to make Randall's drink, and he drinks another shot
in the background.
I go over to the gay couple.

                GAY COUPLE

We were hoping you'd be here. We wanted to tell you
that we've been together for six months and are moving
in together. Thank you for introducing us.

                    ME

I let you get by? Congratulations.
(turning toward the bar and spoken loudly)
Lyle, can you please get them a drink to celebrate and
put it on my tab? I'm going outside. Thank you.
I immediately went to my "breathing-room area"—the low-rise brick
wall. Usually, I love to sit on the wall and enjoy a beautiful night,
but that night, I was embarrassed and ashamed I was *still* single. And
then, as if paid, while I'm sitting on the wall sulking at my situation,
a young male stranger comes over to me.

                  STRANGER

Can I take your picture so I can jerk off to it later?
Immediately, my self-esteem was boosted.

                    ME

Sure, in that case, take two!
I proudly pose for the guy and he walks off. As I sit on the brick
wall, I have to laugh at the absurdity of it all, especially noting how

quickly my attitude has brightened. For the first time I realize how the bodybuilders must enjoy the attention they get.

Then, unexpectedly, an ex-boyfriend walks up to me. I had heard he'd moved to a much larger city, so I hardly expected to see him at the bar.

GREG

So, Tom, tell me, how did it end between us?
It was an "oh shit" moment, especially as I realized I was trapped like a caged animal talking to him without a savior.

ME

(slowly and carefully choosing my words)
Well, one night you asked me never to call you again.
Click. Two weeks later I called. You said, "Now what did I tell you?" Click.

GREG

Oh, I meant you should never call me using that number.

ME

(disbelieving)
I'm glad you clarified that after all these years.

I found it interesting that Greg approached me years after he had dismissed me. I wish he hadn't, because I wondered for a long time if he only spoke to me because I looked good. Fortunately, Greg didn't hang around that night. You'd think I'd be used to running into exes in such a small city. Regardless, in retrospect, I was quite pleased with how I conducted myself. I must admit when we did break up, I jokingly said I would have rather it ended with me as a widow! Not really, but it was effective at changing the conversation topic when my friends asked prying questions about our relationship.

I smile now when I think of the time that guy wanted my picture. However, there was a not-so-funny incident that occurred during this period. One night, I was alone at the bar eating my chicken when this strange, somewhat heavyset guy came over. From just his appearance you could see he was odd, but, truth be told, most of us are odd in one way or another. So the guy started asking me questions and wouldn't stop. After a while, I got the sense he was more interested in getting my attention than in my answers. Since it was early evening, and the bar area was deserted, I was stuck with this guy. Finally, with the meal finished, I said I needed some air, and he followed me outside. Once outside, and in the company of other people from adjacent small businesses in the shared smoking area, he decided to leave, much to my delight and relief. I watched him get into a bright blue vehicle with a distinct black and gray pinstripe and drive out of the parking lot.

A few days later, I was walking from my house to my car in the driveway. To my shock and horror, that same vehicle was driving by! This could not be a coincidence. It was very upsetting that somehow he found out where I lived. Scared and nervous, I got in my car and drove around the block. I passed him and confirmed it was him driving the car.

I decided it would be best to go to the gym where there were other people. I wasn't in the gym but a minute, and I was standing at the front counter with the gym manager when, upsettingly, the guy walked in!

In front of the manager, I said to the guy in my best thug-like voice, "You have no business here."

I doubt if my vocal imitation would win an Academy Award, but I made my point. From the corner of my eye, I saw that the gym manager was surprised. Arrogantly, the guy said he was there for a tour.

With a straight arm, I pointed toward the door, and, in a slow, deep voice I hadn't used previously or since, I commanded, "GET OUT. IF YOU EVER COME BACK I WILL CALL THE POLICE."

Fortunately, the guy turned around left the gym without any hesitation or resistance. Luckily, I never saw him or his vehicle again. Through it all, the gym manager stood there in disbelief during the entire event. Sometimes you gotta do what you gotta do.

59 P-Lee Ends

Through all the training with Lee, I had difficulty deciding how to best show Lee that he was loved and how that love would help him get over his issues. It preoccupied me seemingly forever. Even with all those gym people inquiring about his health and the efforts of those I recruited, I wasn't seeing any results. Then came the day of a harsh realization, when I learned my mistake.

> As my last bodybuilding session is nearing conclusion, Lee and I are walking toward a machine. I have a sanitizing wipe in my hand.
>
> ME
>
> You know, it's great being driven and goal oriented. But don't strive for trophies, strive for friendships. What use are the trophies when you are old? They can't talk or help you when you are down or lonely. Plus, you've got to dust them. Trophies are of no value unless you can sit on them.
>
> I was surprised by Lee's response.
>
> LEE
>
> Well, I don't know, some of them …
>
> Lee stops at a machine. He starts adjusting the weight as I wipe it off.

When helping people, I believe it's best to let the individuals formulate their own decisions since, after all, they are the subject matter experts on themselves. I merely try to provide them with the tools or a perspective to enable them to draw their own objective conclusion. By formulating their own decisions/conclusions, I feel they are more likely to act upon them. However, out of frustration and desperation, and after months of failed efforts, uncharacteristically and against my beliefs, I told Lee "the deal."

ME

You have some wonderful friends. I'm sure you appreciate them. They were very worried about you when you were going through your divorce. Life is about love, and your friends love you. I've said it several times: you're a lucky man.

I sit on the machine.

LEE

(ignoring my conversation)
Give me fifteen.

As I am performing the fifteen reps, Lee continues talking.

Life is about control.

Eight, nine, ten …

After finishing the fifteen repetitions, I speak.

ME

(acting surprised)
Control?
Look, your friends love you and just want you happy.
They don't know how to make that happen.

Lee didn't provide any additional response to my comments. Perhaps he didn't care what his friends thought. Or maybe, since he knew I was friendly with his friends, he wondered what they had discussed with me. Since Lee didn't know what I had orchestrated with P-Lee, it's possible he hadn't understood me. Only Lee knows for sure.

One thing was certain: when Lee said that life is about control, I realized that Lee and I had a fundamental difference about how we view life. I believe that life is about love, not control. As a result of our fundamental difference, I realize P-Lee was doomed to fail. I may be naïve, but until Lee spoke those words, it never occurred to me that life was about anything other than love. With P-Lee, the important warrior lesson is to ensure the basis of our projects and all related efforts fall within the fundamental beliefs of those we seek to help. Otherwise, we are wasting time, effort, and money. Naturally, I learned the lesson the hard way. With this new life perspective, I was able to gain a whole new insight into past events with Lee.

And so, with my last bodybuilding session concluded, P-Lee was finished. I was defeated but learned an invaluable lesson.

60 What I Was Thinking

Although the bodybuilding training had concluded, I still had one more posing session with Lee. Certainly, the best was saved for last!

If you don't know what a camel toe is, please search the internet for a picture before you read further.

Prior to the posing session, I was sitting around the gym table finishing my chicken-in-a-bag meal when a few hulking muscle guys, now my friends, joined me.

At the round table.

TROY

Had Elizabeth last night. She took it like a champ.

ME

I taught her well. (everyone laughs).

What happened to your girlfriend, Gonorracocka?

TED

(laughing)

She left. When is your show?

ME

Saturday.

TED

Good luck, man.

ME

Thanks. Last posing session tonight.

A very good-looking male visitor comes over to look at a framed collection of Megan's show pictures lining the wall by the round

table. No doubt he is waiting for his girlfriend to finish training with
Megan.

TROY

Who's tanning you?

ME

Charity auction. Please bid!

Again, everyone laughs. Troy and Ted catch me staring at the good-
looking visitor. They nod and smile at me, which I interpret as "go for
it." So I seize the opportunity.

ME

(to the good-looking visitor)
I hope you don't notice Megan's camel toe in the
pictures.

The visitor looks closer at the picture and appears not to know what
to say. Troy and Ted barely maintain composure.

ME

I'm about to report her to the SPCA for harboring an
exotic animal.

The visitor flushed. Troy and Ted nearly fell out of their chairs
laughing. I remained cool and collected.

Twenty minutes later, Lee, Cheryl, and I are in the posing room for
our last session. As usual, I am grateful that Cheryl is there as a buffer
between Lee and me. It is just the three of us. Surprisingly, Megan
and her girls are not with us in the posing room.

I knew my posing was bad—really bad. Perhaps I could convert some
of the poses into dance and apply for a job as a Rockette. Despite
asking people to help me pose and watching posing videos, it is too
late. To make things worse, tonight Lee's attention isn't on his paying
trainee!

I am in the center of the floor posing to Lee's barked orders. Lee and

Cheryl are sitting together on the floor against the wall, which is about fifteen feet away. Lee's arm is still in a sling from the operation.

Make no mistake, both my leg and eyelid are twitching nonstop, as they have been for the prior two weeks. I am becoming increasingly irritated at Lee's lack of professionalism with every passing minute.

LEE

When they call out a new pose, don't be too quick to execute it. You need to hesitate. You don't want to be the first. One-quarter turn.

I rotate by ninety degrees.

(to Cheryl)

That's a pretty dress. Glad you wore it.

(spoken harsher and louder)

Tom, you've got to stop using the mirrors to validate your poses. One-quarter turn.

I rotate.

CHERYL

I want to look my best in church. I was going to change after church. You like it?

LEE

(smiles at Cheryl)

One-quarter turn.

I perform another one-quarter turn. By now I am boiling mad. There is little doubt the "unpleasant" Tom will soon appear.

LEE

Maybe I should start going to your church.

(spoken louder)

One-quarter turn.

(to Cheryl)

I would like to wake up next to you in the morning.

Upon hearing those words, I gave up on Lee as a trainer and lost all hope that he would or could help me correct my poor posing. Ever since the time I threw up twice and blew up at Lee, I had bitten my tongue, looked the other way, and compensated for his coaching deficiencies. I had reached the end of my patience. Then, as if scripted, Cheryl asked him a question.

CHERYL

I wonder what Tom is thinking?

ME

(nonchalantly and honestly)

Actually, I was just wondering how many guys went wrong with Lee.

Everyone is silent. It is a very tense moment. I remain in posing position in the middle of the floor. I was actually questioning how many guys were disappointed with Lee's training. Most people, including Lee and Cheryl, would not have translated it that way. Lee's face turns beet red, and he looks like he wants to kill me. Perhaps if his arm wasn't in a sling, he would have tried something.

ME

(feeling rather relieved and speaking calmly)

Well, I thought it was funny.

I more than made my point. Cheryl quickly and accurately assesses the situation.

CHERYL

I'm sorry. I've been a distraction. Tom's right, we need to concentrate on his posing.

ME

You know, Lee, I think it'll be best if I go to the show alone. I'll be fine there without a trainer.

I wondered if he would have been so distracted if Megan had been in the room. Maybe Megan was trying to help me and having her join us all those weeks was really to my benefit.

I felt bad telling Lee not to go to the show. Quite frankly, I couldn't see him contributing anything positive, and I certainly didn't need any more distractions or stress. I knew it would take all my concentration and courage to pull this off—exponentially more than required for that football throw test in high school PE.

61 It's Up to Me

Truthfully, I had no clue how I was going to pull this show off. The twelve weeks of spending three hours a day at the gym, plus working full time, performing household tasks, Tina's funeral, and doing food preparation had taken its toll on me. Similar to the pregnant and exhausted-looking Jennifer at work, I too had reached my limits—as was evident in my tired appearance and less-than-optimistic attitude. I wish I could say I had plan B ready to execute, but I didn't. And I was too worn down to think of something. The reality of spending weeks focusing on Project Lee and not solely improving my posing was now staring me in the face. I knew I didn't have to do the show, but I really wanted to.

The show was Saturday, and I took off work Thursday and Friday to prepare. My final posing session with Lee had been Wednesday night. Now it was all up to me.

I spent all day Thursday practicing my posing. In fact, I was practicing to a posing video in my living room when the phone rang.

ME

Hello.

JANICE

Ready to head to Hartford?

ME

Not really. I was just practicing posing.

JANICE

Has it improved?

ME

No. It's pretty bad. This is going to be worse than the
time I shot the ball into the basket for the opposing
team when I was eight. I hope I don't cry like I did
then.

JANICE

I forgot to tell you. The spray tan will ruin the hotel
towels and sheets, so take your own.

ME

Thanks for letting me know. I plan to take my DVD
player and boom box so I can practice in the room.
Anything else you think I need?

JANICE

No, you're good.

ME

You know, the one thing I've realized through this
bodybuilding is how much influence the Women in the
Church organization has.

JANICE

What do you mean?

ME

Well, I've been paying more attention in the grocery
store, and it seems many items are WIC qualified.

JANICE

Tom, WIC is a food-assistance program, not Women in
the Church!

ME

Oh.

CONNOR

Hey, man. Best wishes for the show.

ME

Thanks. I'll need it.

CONNOR

I know. I've watched Lee train guys for years. He doesn't

get involved. You get what he gives himself. No more,
no less. You either get it or you don't. Either way, it's not
his problem.

ME

There is a big difference between training me and
training himself.

CONNOR

Just act confident.

ME

(matter-of-factly)
I don't have any reason to have any confidence.

And I certainly didn't. Sad but true.

The plan for Friday and Saturday was simple. On Friday, I would practice posing in the gym for a few hours, pack up the car, and head to Hartford late in the afternoon. The competition on Saturday would have two
distinct parts. In the morning competition, we would appear before the
judges in groups. Saturday night was the show. Generally, it's the night
event that attracts the competitor's friends and family—and brings in the
profit for the show's organizers.

Although we are judged during both the morning and evening venues,
the majority of the scoring is done in the morning. One big difference between the sessions is that each contestant is allocated one minute to pose by
himself in the evening. Brian had suggested I pose to a song called "Warrior" by Bellevue Underground—the same song John listened to during
the night when he was battling cancer.

I wasn't familiar with the song, but I made a one-minute clip of it
for posing during the evening program. Even during posing practice, I
was concentrating on the poses and not on the lyrics. During the drive to
Hartford I decided to play the whole song. I was so haunted by the lyrics,
I played the song repeatedly and fell in love with it. Some of the lyrics go
like this:

I know you're scared and a little shy

Too afraid to show the real you inside
So you've built a wall that you hide behind
A wall that's so tall, not even you can climb
…

Your friends see you and think what a shame
There are those who claim your childhood is to blame
But a warrior will fight, without fear or respite
For battles of the mind, victory is hard to find

"Warrior" (www.thatwarrior.com) so well summarized my situation with Lee and with so many others I know.

Fortunately, I booked a room at the show's sponsoring hotel, and this greatly eased competition registration and attendance at the mandatory Friday night six o'clock meeting. During the meeting, show representatives went over our Saturday schedule and asked us to fill out a survey. We had to pass a lie detector test to prove we did not consume any performance-enhancing drugs. Those of us who purchased the spray tanning option, myself included, listened to an overview of the tanning procedure and day-of-show process, and we waited to have our initial full-body tan applied prior to going to bed.

It was late Friday night when I returned to my hotel room. To help relieve my show fear, I watched a bodybuilding show video to better understand what I would experience the next day. It seemed simple enough.

On Saturday, it was an early drive to the venue where the contest would take place. The event officials explained the proceedings in detail, including the morning and evening venues. Mandatory participation in both venues makes for a very long day.

While seated in the show venue Saturday morning, I met an insightful competitor. He said it's helpful to practice posing behind the stage while waiting for the show to start. So we went behind the stage. Almost immediately, he started making suggestions to improve my posing. Too embarrassed to tell him I had paid a posing instructor, I acted like I learned posing by myself from videos. He certainly didn't doubt me.

Somehow, I got through the morning competition, it was mostly a blur. But I vividly recall feeling relaxed over my posing trunk appearance anxiety after I checked out the other guys and noted I had seen more pronounced camel toe. Before long I found I was really enjoying myself.

62 The Late Show

In the evening I was energized knowing my friends Vanessa, Judy, Cynthia, Howard, and Sheila were in the audience to cheer me on. Since the morning competition went without serious embarrassment, there was nothing to worry about for the evening competition. I was having fun as a competitor, and it occurred to me that I wouldn't be enjoying myself nearly as much as a spectator.

The venue was packed. From the side of the stage I see people of all ages. I unsuccessfully scan the audience for my friends. Freshly spray tanned to the shade of tea and standing in line with the other competitors behind the stage.

ANNOUNCER
From Pawtucket, Rhode Island, number 6, Thomas Caesar. He writes, "Prolonged viewing may burn your retinas."

"Warrior" by Bellevue Underground starts playing from the auditorium speakers. With my body on autopilot as I practiced it many times before, I begin the one-minute posing routine.

From the audience I can hear my friends cheering for me.

63 Another Battle Over

It is strange how miracles occur. I'd gone from a failed basketball start to an amazing fourth-place finish in the bodybuilding competition. Maybe it wasn't a miracle but rather the outcome of believing in myself and tapping into that inner strength I didn't know existed.

There weren't any tears—of either joy or embarrassment. I've been told it's impressive to place in your first show. Perhaps so, but I'd exchange my trophy for Lee to realize his life is about love and that he is loved. That is the reason I trained in the first place. I am, however, proud of my show placement and thankful I pulled it all together.

As planned, I departed on that sixteen-day transatlantic "reward" cruise right after the show. It was hardly a party cruise—I spent an enormous amount of time in the various spa rooms destressing with the expensive spa pass I purchased. I knew it was money well spent when, on the fourteenth day, both the leg and eyelid twitching ceased for good.

I do recall a memorable laugh. While sunning myself on deck, I opened my eyes to find some guy taking my picture. Not again! After he realized I was awake and had caught him in the act, he explained he thought I was hot! Had he bought me a drink, he could have had not only the picture but also a happy ending.

Between doing the bodybuilding show and taking the trip, I was away from the gym for almost three weeks. Upon my return to xCellFitness and within minutes of arriving, I was most impressed when Neal, who originally questioned my training and probably didn't see much bodybuilding potential in me, came over to congratulate me. I could tell he really meant it. And yes, he paid back all the money he borrowed. That is one classy guy.

As for Lee, well, occasionally I run into him. Seldom do we exchange more than pleasantries, if that. Sometimes I wonder if his miracle ever happened. Oh well, maybe tomorrow. But I do wish him all the best. I don't hold any grudges toward him over my training experience. My expectations were probably too high, something I've been working on for years. I am most proud that while other people criticized and talked about him, I was a man of action. I tried to help—just as my country music heroes would have done. Knowing the outcome, would I do it again? Absolutely. Of the four people I recruited to help, only one asked me how I made out. Seriously, though, I hope Lee's walls fall soon.

My neighbors, Sheila and Howard, keep me in check. Besides the frequent yard chats, a few times a year we have neighbor dinners—usually at Sheila's house—where we catch up and hurl one-liners at each other. For years, I yelled, "Ass to the house!" across the street to Sheila while she gardened in sundresses, but no longer. Not long ago her boyfriend moved in with her, and she completely changed her yard-work attire. Immediately there was a lot less traffic on our street. And it's much quieter too. Who knows, one day I just may yell "ass to the house" just to see if I get a reaction. Maybe one day Sheila will yell it at me!

Sheila's dog, Jack, became a best bud and remained so until the day he died. I loved how he'd bark to let me know he was available for a visit. He was most contented with the hearty pettings he frequently got. I like to think both our lives became so much fuller by knowing each other. Yes, the way to a canine's heart is through his stomach. At least it was for Jack.

As can happen with friends, my friendship with Connor and Janice faded. They were so instrumental in unselfishly aiding me through the bodybuilding training. For that I am extremely grateful. Perhaps one day our lives' journeys will once again unite. Until then I wish them the best.

Similarly, both Vanessa and Judy moved away from the area in opposite directions. Often I see Judy's social media postings. Less often Vanessa and I text.

Victoria got the professional help she needed, which resulted in her leaving the gym and consequently exiting our lives. Despite missing her, it was a smart move for her and I admire and applaud her strength in fighting her demons. Victoria still remains one of the most beautiful people I've ever met and a standard by which I judge beauty. I hope that, during the storms of life, she remembers to smile and put her best girl forward.

It brings a smile to my face when I recall that whole "naked picture" story with Jay requesting them from Victoria. Sadly, Jay passed away. He was a good guy. I wish I could have attended his funeral. He's probably watching us from above just shaking his head.

Barbara closed the bar. But it was never just a bar—it was a safe, clean, drug-free place where you could go as-is or as-you-wanted-to-be. Either way, you were wanted, encouraged, loved, protected, and accepted. It's too bad there aren't more places like that. Most people I know who did a bodybuilding show thought the training and dieting was a huge deal; I'll be the first to admit it was hard. But it's much harder to expose the inner you and defy society's expectations. The real strength lies in the individuals at that bar, not those in the gym. Upon the bar's closing, I sent Barbara a thank-you card for the love and outstanding service she provided to our community.

Last I heard, Brian is training people. I am proud of my role in encouraging him to obtain his personal trainer certification. He hasn't contacted me since being insulted over my flashing comments and going into isolation. Oh well, what gay person isn't colorful? I heard he straightened himself out. Everyone deserves a second chance and like several of my country music heroes, I'm glad he seized the opportunity. I couldn't be prouder of him. He has a lot of good in him, and I am happy he selected such a noble profession.

A few years after Tina's death, Rich married one of their longtime friends, Carol. Once again laughter and love echo through the halls of that magical house. I am delighted for them, and I cherish the time I spend with them. Of all the wonderful people who have departed my life, I miss Tina the most and think about her constantly. She would have loved this book and its message; I witnessed her living its philosophy.

With his full mobility, whenever I see Josh I am reminded that miracles happen every day. Coincidentally enough, we always seem to bump into each other just when I need a spiritual lift. By now he recognizes me, and we always have a nice chat. I am so glad he remained in the area.

And finally, my dear friend Cynthia: we still meet occasionally and laugh hysterically. Remember that guy she met? Well, it worked out, and they've been happily together for several years—they even bought a house together. Who'd have thought? Best of all, she caught him without having a snip, tuck, or lift performed! Just as in the beginning of our friendship, she keeps me sane in a make-up-your-own-reality world. Life is wonderful having someone loving enough to tell me what I need to hear and loving enough not to be upset if I don't act upon it.

After the bodybuilding show, I kept up rigorous training for about a year. Without a bodybuilding goal, I gradually stopped working out and did not maintain a healthy diet. Looking at me today, it appears that I've eaten the weights I once lifted. I am back to looking like the "before" photo. But I am jollier. Dennis, the wise sage, says he's going to get me back into shape. I hope it happens soon, before I start wearing my shower curtain! Just being around Dennis brings a great calmness over me, it would be an honor to be trained by him.

I moved on and developed other hobbies. What you are reading is the result of one of them.

Since I was a teenager, I've been sending letters and cards to my hero, Loretta Lynn. As I got older, I started sending her flowers. Recently I sent her flowers to thank her for the decades of entertainment and for being such an important influence in my life. I added that I wished I could send her the gold or diamonds I felt she deserved, but I could only afford flowers. Much to my delight, I heard she loved the flowers.

Sadly, I never have been anyone's destination for a long-term, meaningful relationship. I refuse to settle—I've known many couples with great relationships, so I recognize the chemistry that must exist between two people to have them. I've discounted myself quite a bit over the years, but I refuse to discount myself for a relationship. The time has come to focus less on casual acquaintances and more on those with whom I might possibly share my life. I need to do this for me; I don't think I'm being selfish. Perhaps some other warrior can fill my void.

And speaking of warriors, isn't it time you join us? Why not? You won't have to diet, perform bodybuilding poses, look like an "after photo," or spend any money. Start by focusing on the Manners characteristic and apply one positive improvement to your regular interactions with people, such as:

- Treat others like you want to be treated (with respect).

- Put yourself in someone else's shoes.

- If you don't have anything nice to say, say nothing at all.

- Speak only on behalf of yourself.

- A smile, a little encouragement, or a kind gesture (such as opening a door) goes a long way.

- Nobody ever looked better by making someone else look bad.

- Listen to what others are saying.

- Don't provide an opinion or recommendation unless asked.

- *Don't hold others to your standards, views, tastes or lifestyle.*

If you do only that as a result of reading my book, thank you. I will consider my efforts on this book successful. As you can tell from my dialogue, like most people I struggle with this Manners characteristic. I never claimed to be perfect—only firm! So we can both work on it together! As you build confidence and perfect your technique, increase the improvements and add additional warrior characteristics as necessary or desired. You will make such a difference in the lives of others with unimaginable satisfaction in yours.

The next time a male stranger holds the door open for you, it may be me, *that warrior.*

As the great Loretta Lynn sings, "We've Come A Long Way, Baby"! She has. I have. And so will you.

Acknowledgments

You know, the life's wonderful journey has many roads to walk. Sometimes the roads I picked weren't paved or fastest to my destination. Whether the right or wrong road, the walk was fun and rewarding through the love shared among the amazing people that I walked with. And included with the amazing people are my country music heroes who constantly remind me to work hard, be honest, persevere, and to be nice. And maybe someone considers me amazing. I applaud those individuals who found me worthy to receive their love and support. For this effort, I would like to acknowledge:

Thank you to Cassandra Dutrey-Ellis for her unyielding friendship.
Thank you to DiFiori Design for their expert design consultation and patience. Contact them at: www.difioridesign.com
Author's bio photo courtesy of photographer Lori Gibbons-Munn.
Back cover photo courtesy of wildlife photographer Linda Orr.

Permission granted to quote from the following (All Rights Reserved):
"Warrior" by Jeffrey S. Marshall and Richard S. Johnson
Copyright © 2013 Jeffrey S. Marshall and Richard S. Johnson.
"You Ain't Woman Enough (To Take My Man)" by Loretta Lynn
Copyright Sure Fire Music Company Inc.

Last, but not least, my country music heroes who have been inspiring me since the age of thirteen: Loretta Lynn, Conway Twitty, Tammy Wynette, George Jones, Dolly Parton, Reba McEntire, and Tanya Tucker. No matter where I go, you are always with me. Thank you.

About The Author

Thomas M. Caesar

Best-selling authors such as Danielle Steel, John Grisham, Clive Cussler, and Stephen King need not fear competition from Thomas M Caesar. Thomas is a self-proclaimed international male sex symbol who has never written anything more substantial than an occasional Christmas letter. He lists the tabloids as his favorite reading material. Whether for a good laugh or a buck, Thomas divulges his innermost revelations gained from his forty plus years of living—no small feat for a man whose vocabulary is limited to mostly four-letter words, especially those words which can be expressed with an accompanying finger gesture, his preferred method of communication.

Even though Thomas's neighbors may consider him the crazy "cat lady," he has traveled extensively and considers himself fortunate to share his life's wonderful journey with amazing people and astonishing pets. He can be spotted in his car singing duets with his country music heroes. Most of his friends agree that Thomas is a nice guy. His favorite activities, laughing and making people laugh, come easily and frequently to Thomas. At present Thomas is living in Wilmington, Delaware.

Made in the USA
Middletown, DE
07 December 2024